CARTBOY
and the
TIME
CAPSULE

CARTBOY
and the
TIME
CAPSULE

L. A. Campbell

A Tom Doherty Associates Book
New York

CARTBOY AND THE TIME CAPSULE

Copyright © 2013 by L. A. Campbell

A Starscape Book
Published by Tom Doherty Associates, LLC
175 Fifth Avenue
New York, NY 10010

www.tor-forge.com

Library of Congress Cataloging-in-Publication Data

Campbell, L. A., 1962–
     Cartboy and the time capsule / L.A. Campbell.—First edition.
        p. cm.
     "A Tom Doherty Associates Book."
     ISBN 978-0-7653-3317-9 (paper over board)
     ISBN 978-1-4668-0201-8 (e-book)
     1. History—Fiction.   2. Fathers and sons—Fiction.
  3. Schools—Fiction.   4. Diaries—Fiction.   5. Humorous
  stories.   I. Title.
  PZ7.C15478Car 2013
  [Fic]—dc23

                                                    2012043358

Starscape books may be purchased for educational, business, or promotional use. For information on bulk purchases, please contact Macmillan Corporate and Premium Sales Department at 1-800-221-7945 extension 5442 or write specialmarkets@macmillan.com.

First Edition: April 2013

To Ian

CARTBOY

and the

TIME CAPSULE

Hello, Greetings, Zip Dop Smirg!

My name is Hal Rifkind.

I'm not sure "zip dop smirg" is how you say hi to someone who lives in the future, but I figured it was worth a try.

I'm not even sure if you are a kid or a human. You could be a robot. Or an android. Or an alien from a planet that hasn't been discovered.

All I know for sure is, if you are reading this, you found the time capsule. And you live way in the future. Hundreds of years from now. Because that's the earliest Mr. Tupkin said the time capsule would be opened.

Mr. Tupkin is my history teacher. He has white hair and wears suspenders and a bow tie.

The bow tie is a modern-day fashion accessory that automatically makes you look a hundred years older.

Today, he gave our class a *humongous* assignment. Not only was it *huge,* there was no warning whatsoever. And if you ask me, a little heads-up would have been good.

I walked into class thinking it was going to be a normal October day. But the first thing I saw was a giant stack of books on Mr. Tupkin's desk. They were brand new. And thick. And they looked frighteningly like blank journals.

"What are those?" I asked Mr. Tupkin, trying to hide the quiver in my voice.

He picked up one of the journals and tossed it to me. "This, Mr. Rifkind, is how you will make your mark on the world. By writing to someone who lives in the future. And telling them all about the times we live in. Everything about life today."

"Everything?"

"Yes. But don't worry. You have the whole year to do it."

If Mr. Tupkin was telling me there was a homework assignment that lasted the *whole school year,* I had another question.

"Isn't that illegal?"

My best friend, Arnie Gianelli, raised his hand. "What kind of things should we write about, Mr. Tupkin?"

"Think about it. What would *you* want to know about someone who lived in the past? What might be important topics to cover?"

Kids from every corner of the class shouted out ideas.

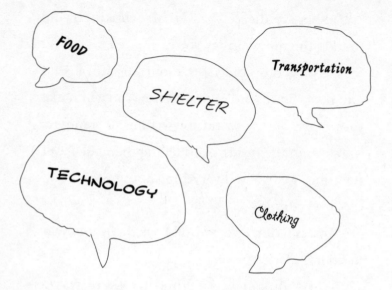

Didn't they see that with every answer they were making the assignment even *longer*?

I, for one, kept my mouth closed.

Mr. Tupkin started passing out the journals to everyone in the class. "You can use pictures you find on the computer," he said, "and you can do drawings. I want you to create several timelines comparing the present to the past."

Timelines? Drawings?

"What if you can't draw?" I asked, trying not to *cry*.

"Do the best you can."

Artist's drawing of a cat.   My drawing of a cat.

"On the last day of school, we'll put all the journals in a time capsule and bury it. Right here in Stowfield, Pennsylvania," said Mr. Tupkin. "On school property. But first, we need to think of a suitable place. A place big enough to hide a large, airtight canister. A place that will not be disturbed for many years."

Mr. Tupkin adjusted his bow tie and pointed to me. "How about you, Mr. Rifkind? Can you think of a spot that is dark and mysterious? Where something could be buried for hundreds of years?"

"Um. The bottom of my locker?"

As with most of my answers in history class, Mr. Tupkin shook his head, sighed, and turned to someone else. He pointed to Cindy Shano, the girl who sits in the front row.

"Cindy. Where should we bury the time capsule?"

"How about under the bleachers by the football field? No one ever goes there."

"Good idea. Under the bleachers it is. We'll put a sign on the time capsule saying that it must stay sealed until at least the year 2500."

If it were up to me, I'd fill the time capsule with Tootsie Pops and Ring Dings. That stuff lasts for centuries.

Mr. Tupkin spent the rest of the class explaining how helpful our time capsule would be to people of the future. How whoever finds our journals will understand history better. And that just by making our journals, we'll understand history better too.

"I promise you," he said right before the bell rang, "you'll get a lot out of this assignment."

Right then, it looked like all I was going to get out of this assignment was a hand cramp, because the rest of the year is a long time to write to someone.

Who might or might not be an alien.

Shelter

Dear Surprised Finder of the Time Capsule
Under the Bleachers:

If you are new to planet Earth and looking for
shelter (a place to live), I have two things to say:

1. Welcome.
2. Do not buy a house with a deck. You
    will live to regret it.

I found this out after I asked my parents for
my own room.

Why does a twelve-year-old boy need his own

room, you might ask. There are lots of reasons, but the top two are called Bea and Perrie. My twin baby sisters. Not only do I share a room with them, my bed is *in between their cribs.*

Between the crying, teething, spit-up, and diapers, I've slept about seven minutes since they were born.

Average size of baby.

Average size of Dumpster that baby fills with pee, poo, and barf.

Needless to say, I've been working on my dad night and day to let me move into the tiny spare room in our house.

"First of all, I need that room for my job" is his usual reply. "And second, the only way I'd consider giving you your own room is if you bring your history grade up. *Way* up."

Judging by how I'm doing in history, it's going to take a miracle. Even though it's only October, Mr. Tupkin has already given us ten pop quizzes and tests. So far, I've gotten the *same grade* on every single one.

HINT: My grade is a letter between *C* and *F*. Words that start with my grade are *Dang, Doomed,* and *Duh.*

"No son of mine will fail history," my dad says every time I bring home a test. "You must do better, Hal. History is who we are and why."

"Boy, do I love history too, Dad. But the thing is, sharing a room with two babies makes it so hard to study. If we had a bigger house . . ."

"Here we go again with the 'bigger house.' You know I work at home. And I've got my whole shop set up in the spare room. It would take months to pack it up. Besides, business is a little slow. There's no way we're moving."

Usually, at some point during the "Hal, you'll never get your own room" speech, I look to my mom for help. But she's got her own "very good" reasons for not getting a bigger house.

"Sharing is nice. You'll establish an everlasting bond with your sisters."

Or: "A small home is greener. Much better for the environment."

And then there's my personal favorite: "If you're feeling tired, honey, I could put some needles in your feet."

That's the other thing about my mom. Her big plan to help out with the family income is to go to night school. She's studying for a degree in acupuncture. It's this Chinese medicine that's popular today.

They say it's been around for thousands of years in China, which I really don't get. Because the idea of acupuncture is to stick needles in people. To make them feel *better.*

My mom practices acupuncture
on our pet rabbit, Scamper.
I am pretty sure Scamper does not like this.

Normally, the conversation about getting my own room ends with me right back where I started. Sitting on my bed, listening to the twins' non-stop jibber-jabber.

The other night, Perrie was trying to talk. She was holding her favorite puppet, a seashell with a hermit crab inside. "Sell. Sell," she said, showing me the shell.

I put my hand inside the shell and made the hermit crab pop out.

"Boo!"

Perrie loves it when I do that. She pointed to the shell again, and said, "Sell."

That's it, I thought. Sell! If only I could sell our house. Get someone to make an offer my parents couldn't refuse.

Sure, they kept telling me they'll never move. But for the right price, maybe my mom and dad would reconsider.

So last Saturday, when my parents said we were going to visit Grampa Janson, I told them I wanted to stay home and study. As soon as they left, I printed out a sign on my computer. It said OPEN HOUSE. It means anyone who's driving by can come in and look at your house to see if they want to buy it. I even decorated the sign for good measure.

For reasons no one understands,
balloons make people go shopping.

Next, I put on a suit I borrowed from Arnie. It was the one he wore to Billy Cohen's bar mitzvah. I have to admit, the suit was a little flashy for me. And not just because I'm not the suit-wearing type.

The thing about Arnie is he actually *likes* dressing up because "girls notice that stuff." The other thing he does is put gel in his hair because it looks "sophisticated."

About half an hour after I put up the OPEN HOUSE sign, I heard a sound that was music to my ears.

Ding-dong.

I opened the door and saw a nice-looking couple standing on the steps.

"Hello, we're here for the open house," said the man.

"Come in."

"Is the homeowner here?"

"He'll be back shortly. In the meantime, why don't I show you around?"

We started to walk through the house and right away the man started firing off questions.

"How close is the nearest school?"

"The Stowfield Middle School is just a stone's throw away, sir."

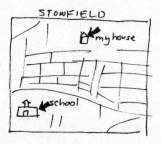

School is really two miles from my house, but I figured if you have a slingshot, it might be a stone's throw away.

The couple walked into our kitchen and looked at the ceiling. "Have you ever had problems with mold?" asked the woman.

"Yes," I said. I figured it was best to be honest. I grabbed a hunk of my dad's favorite blue cheese out of the fridge and tossed it in the trash. "But not anymore."

The man looked me straight in the eye. "Are there any structural issues or deferred payments we should know about?"

Ding-dong. Luckily, I was saved by the bell.

The next people to come to the open house were an older lady and her "friend." After I showed them around a little, I found out her friend was a home inspector.

"I like to bring the inspector with me," said

the lady. "So I'll know if there are problems right off the bat."

The lady and the inspector walked down the hall and stopped in front of the spare room. The one that should be my bedroom right now.

"What's in here?" asked the inspector.

"This room is, um, under renovation," I said, locking the door. "Don't want the dust to get out. Very harmful."

The inspector gave me a look like he knew something was up. But then he turned to the lady, and said, "Why don't we go see the outside of the house?"

As the two of them went to look at our back deck, I stood in front of the spare room. I knew the real reason I didn't want to open that door.

I was embarrassed.

The thing is, the room is filled from floor to ceiling with old microwaves. And DVD players. And toasters from the 1970s. Because my dad's job is fixing appliances.

There are little screws and wires and tools

everywhere, and everything is greasy and dirty. Every time I look in that room I can't help but wonder why it has to be *my dad* who surrounds himself with used stuff. Didn't he ever want anything new, like a normal dad?

I was still standing in front of the door when the inspector suddenly walked up and handed me an official-looking piece of paper. As soon as I saw it, my hands started to sweat. Could this really be it? An offer for the house? I mean, it seemed a bit soon. But if you love a place, you love a place, right?

I stood there holding the paper and I couldn't help but imagine what my new room would look like. Arnie and I would set up RavenCave (the best video game ever). We'd have a special table for chocolate-glazed doughnuts with sprinkles.

The chocolate-glazed doughnut with sprinkles.

The inferior plain doughnut.

Beware of muffins. They are usually mushed-up whole wheat bread in a deceptive cupcake shape.

I was lost in the thought of where the doughnut table would go when I heard the inspector say, "You have a violation. Code one-thirteen. Section nine. Deck railing."

"Thank you. Um, what?"

"Your deck railing is not built to code. The rails are five inches apart. They need to be four. Judging by the toys lying around everywhere, I'm guessing small children live in this house."

"Small children. Yes, two."

"Young man, I'd fix that deck if you want those children to be safe. And if you want to avoid a fine."

Things my dad likes doing more than paying fines:

Boiling in oil.

Getting eaten by a mountain lion.

It wasn't until later in the day that my family got back from Grampa Janson's. My dad was pretty surprised to see me on the back deck.

"Haven't seen you holding a hammer in years, son."

"I just want to make sure Bea and Perrie don't fall off the deck. These rails are a little far apart, don't you think, Dad? What do you say we fix them together?"

"That's my boy! Why buy new when you can fix the old!"

I spent the first two weeks of October working on the deck, thinking about how I'd never have my own room.

And how I'd be spending the rest of my life next to two girls who have five teeth between them.

A Timeline of Man's Attemp

o Get a Roof Over His Head

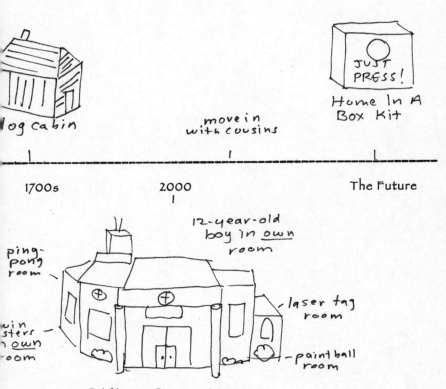

log cabin

move in
with cousins

JUST
PRESS!

Home In A
Box Kit

| 1700s | 2000 | The Future |

ping-
pong
room

12-year-old
boy in own
room

laser tag
room

...in
...sters
...n own
...oom

paintball
room

The Hal Rifkind Dream McMansion

Transportation

If you are from a galaxy outside our solar system, you probably came here by a light beam–powered rocket, like the kind they have on Realm III (a video game about space travel). Or maybe you were transkinetically teleported, in which case I hope you were wearing shin guards.

If you're a human, I'm guessing your "car" runs on cow manure or melted candy corns 'cause that's the way things are going. All I know is if there's one thing people are always trying to improve, it's the way they travel around.

Today, the most amazing form of transportation is something called the Ziptuk E300S Motorized Scooter. Basically, it can take you anywhere you need to go. Like from home to school, or from the couch to the fridge.

I hope the E300S is still around when you are reading this.
And that you have no more than two legs.

I first saw one on a television show called *Grombits 2020*. It was about a kid who has to escape from these half-werewolf, half-snake creatures. He jumped from one rooftop to another one that was like, eighty feet away. All the kid had to do was stand on his Ziptuk E300S, press a button, and, *kapow,* he was on the other roof in seconds.

Another thing that makes the Ziptuk the most exciting form of transportation known to humans today is that you don't need a driver's license to use one. Which is especially good news for someone like me since my parents make me walk to school two miles each way. They say it's because walking is greener.

The green movement was the best thing that ever happened to my parents, because we were suddenly walking everywhere to "save the Earth" instead of to save three dollars on gas.

Recycled toilet paper is very green.
I'm not sure why anyone would want used toilet paper.

I knew I had to have a Ziptuk E300S, but convincing my parents to buy me one would be impossible because A) They cost a lot of money and B) They cost a lot of money. Even though I had practically memorized the E300S's brochures and commercials, I wasn't going to try to talk my parents into it.

But then, last week, Mr. Tupkin gave us a truly mind-melting test. It was on George Washington, Thomas Jefferson, and James Madison. We were supposed to know what each of them contributed to America's independence.

I actually did study. Or at least I tried to. I Googled (looked up stuff on the Internet)

Thomas Jefferson brought French fries to America.

George Washington only had one tooth.

"Fathers of the U.S." and found some pretty interesting facts.

I guess it wasn't too surprising that none of those little nuggets of information appeared on the test, and my grade was another D.

After the bell rang, Mr. Tupkin announced that a few of us needed to do some extra work to catch up. The few of us turned out to be just me.

"You nearly failed another test, Mr. Rifkind. "You must relearn the material, and take it again. For it is history that teaches us the future."

"I see what you're saying, Mr. Tupkin, about the past and the future and barely passing the test and all," I said. "But last night was super tricky for studying. You may not know this, but I share a room with a pair of teething toddlers. So I went to Arnie's house to study for the test, but we got slightly distracted by RavenCave. Seeing as how we're trying to get to Level Thirteen . . ."

Sadly, the words fell on deaf ears. (Literally, Mr. Tupkin is deaf in one ear.) He loaded me up with four hours of homework and three text-books that weigh about six pounds each.

How kids lug home books these days.
Weight Limit: 15 pounds.
Daily Homework: 45 pounds.

Normally, I would've wanted to throw up. But then I realized this just might be a good thing. All those extra books could be my chance to get what I needed most in the world besides my own room.

As soon as I got home from school I yelled for my dad. "Dad! I think I dislocated my shoulder!"

"Let me see!" he said, running into the kitchen.

"Here, grab my backpack first."

I threw the backpack in my dad's direction. *Clonk!* It landed so hard on the kitchen floor it might as well have been full of bricks.

"Hal! This backpack is way too heavy for you."

"I know! I better get a Ziptuk E300S scooter. The brochure says it's a totally wireless transporter that intuitively moves where my body tells it to."

"Yes, I agree. What did you say?"

My dad is a little on the slow side. But I could see the wheels spinning in his head while he was trying to come up with a solution. Which, when it comes to my dad, is not usually a good thing. 'Cause the other habit he has is coming up with these crazy money-saving schemes and tricks.

Finally, after an eternity, he looked at me like he had just invented bread. "Son, you do need a transporter that's easy to move. I'll be right back."

Just as I was picturing the pangs of jealousy I'd be seeing in the other kids at school, and thinking that once I got the Ziptuk's handling down, I might give Arnie a ride, I looked up to see my dad stroll into the kitchen. He was wheeling a squeaky blue metal cart.

"You're in luck!" my dad said. "Mrs. Cavanaugh finally moved to the retirement community. She won't be needing this beauty anymore. The wheels turn fine and the squeaks are barely audible. I got it for a song."

"Don't you think I might look a little ridiculous pushing a cart that one-hundred-year-old ladies use to carry fruit?"

"I'm going to insist you take it to school whenever you have lots of homework, Hal. Like you said, you don't want to risk a shoulder injury, or a slipped disc, or one of those pesky groin pulls. . . ."

"Dad. Think about what the other kids will say."

"Safety first," he said. "Bad backs run in our family and this will protect you. I don't want you to end up all hunched over like some of your relatives."

↑
Uncle Lou

In the end, I agreed to take the cart to school. Mostly because when my dad gets an idea in his head, there's no changing his mind. Plus, I figured, maybe if I gave in on something, he would too. Like giving me my own room sometime in the next *decade*.

The next day, Arnie helped me pull the cart from my house to school. I'm pretty lucky to have him as a friend. We've known each other since we were little kids, I mean really little. Like, our moms have pictures of us together in the bathtub when we were three.

I guess that's the main reason I stick with him. That, and if I'm not nice to him, he might put those bathtub pictures up on the Internet.

After a few days of dragging the cart around the halls of middle school, I started to get used to my new nickname, Cartboy. About half the kids call me that now, especially Arnie's older brother, Garth, and his eighth-grade buddies.

HEY CARTBOY, CARRY MY BOOKS!

Cartboy, can I borrow some denture cream?

HOW ARE THE GRANDKIDS, CARTBOY?

Which brings me to the question I've been meaning to ask you. Seeing as how you live in the future, do you happen to have a time machine handy? Something that could zap me out of here? Get me to a different place? Anywhere far from Stowfield?

If so, would you mind beaming me up?

Because between my dad, Mr. Tupkin, and the eighth-graders at Stowfield, I don't see how I'm going to make it through sixth grade.

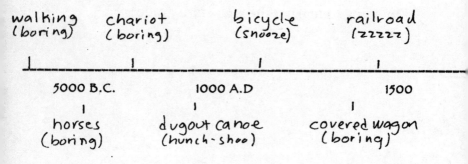

walking   chariot   bicycle   railroad
(boring)   (boring)   (snooze)   (zzzzz)

| 5000 B.C. | 1000 A.D | 1500 |

horses   dugout canoe   covered wagon
(boring)   (hunch-shoo)   (boring)

Transportation

RV
(boring)

Intergalactic Voice—
Activated Flying Saucer
(not so boring)

|_____|_____

2000   The Future

car
boring)

The Ziptuk E300S!!!
Perfect for Stunts!!!
Makes a great gift !!!

Super-sized deck and frame

Easily removable seat for stand-up riding

High-performance chain-driven motor

Speeds up to 15 mph

10" pneumatic tires for a smooth ride

Adjusting handlebars

Twist-grip acceleration control

Padded seat

Retractable kickstand

Rechargeable battery

Handlebar folding mechanism

Sports

Dear Alien/Person/Possible Humanoid/Robot:

One thing about living in the future that must be *fantastic* is that you probably have highly developed techniques for staying awake in history class. Like, maybe you can inject history facts directly into your brain so you don't have to memorize them.

I could have really used those injections today.

Mr. Tupkin went on for *thirty-five minutes* about colonies and declarations and proclamations and stuff.

"In the 1700s, many colonists living in this country wanted to break away from British rule," he said. "For them, the need for freedom was the most important thing in the world. So important, they were willing to trade their lives for it."

He walked toward the back of the classroom and stopped dangerously close to my desk. "For your time-capsule journals, I want you to describe what you think is the most important thing happening in the world today. How about you, Mr. Rifkind? Do you know the most important thing happening in the world?"

"Yes, sir, I do."

"Superb. What is it?"

"Sports."

Once again, Mr. Tupkin turned straight from me to Cindy Shano.

"Cindy, how about you?"

"I would say the United Nations' efforts to achieve peace throughout the world."

If you have ever been to a Yankees–Red Sox game,
you know that peace throughout the world is not possible.

"Good answer," said Mr. Tupkin. As he walked back to his desk, he shot me a look. "That should have been your answer, Mr. Rifkind."

It's not that I don't think world peace is important. I do. I just don't see how Mr. Tupkin and Cindy Shano could overlook these riveting statistics:

- The Philadelphia Eagles (best football team in the world), for the first time in like ninety years, are undefeated.

- If the Philadelphia Flyers (best hockey team in the world) trade Riley Cote, they have a decent shot at the cup.

- The Phillies (best baseball team in the world) are two and one in the series.

My favorite sport is baseball, which I love to play. But there are other sports at Stowfield that are very popular too.

1. Being chased by guys who are bigger than you.
2. Getting gum off your locker that was put there by guys who are bigger than you.
3. Doing stuff you don't want to do because guys bigger than you said to do it.

By guys who are bigger than you, I'm pretty much talking about Garth and his buddies Ryan Horner and Warren the Wedgiemeister. The guys doing the running would be Arnie and me.

Just about every time we sit down in Arnie's basement to play RavenCave, either Ryan or Garth opens the door and yells down the stairs, "Go get us some sodas, dipwads." Whenever Garth and his friends tell Arnie and me to do something, it usually leaves one option: do it, or else.

The worst one of Garth's friends, by far, is Ryan Horner. And if you're worse than Warren the Wedgiemeister, a heartless savage known for giving sixth-graders up to five wedgies a day, that's saying a lot.

The wedgie: as popular today as it ever was.
If I had to guess, I'd say it's alive and well in your time too.

Ryan knows how hard Arnie and I have been trying to reach Level 13 of RavenCave, and that the key is getting Susie to find the scythe. He stands over us and says, "I'll tell you where the scythe is if you get me a Gatorade." He's done it a million times.

Arnie and I made the pact to find the scythe together on the first day of school. Since then, we have looked in *every corner of the cave*. Behind the stalagmites. Inside the treasure chest. On the bottom of the lake.

It's just about killing us. The other thing that's just about killing us is the fact that Ryan Horner constantly rubs it in our faces that he's found the scythe and we haven't.

I'm not surprised the scythe is shaped
like a question mark.
Because that thing is <u>nowhere</u> to be found.

But as soon as we bring Ryan the Gatorade, he just laughs, and says something like, "Should've gotten it faster."

So Arnie and I were pretty shocked when this afternoon, Ryan came down to the basement and asked us in this nice voice we had never heard before, "Do you guys want to play baseball?"

"You mean, like, you want us to be the bases?" Arnie asked.

"Ha, that's cute. No, we just need you and Cartboy to round out the teams."

"No tricks?" I asked.

"Nah. C'mon. We're in the backyard."

Garth, the Wedgiemeister, and a bunch of their friends were waiting. We divided up the teams, but before we got started, Garth said, "There's just one rule." He looked at Arnie and me. "Newcomers have to get the ball from the neighbor's yard if it goes in."

"That's not what we agreed to . . ."

"Keep your lid on, Cartboy, it hardly ever happens."

"Yeah, Wolfie never bites," said Ryan with a weird smile. "Well, hardly ever."

Arnie was up at bat first, and while he was busy missing every pitch, I stood in the outfield wondering who Wolfie was.

After Arnie struck out, the Wedgiemeister walked up to the plate. He took a swing and *kaboom*! The ball went over the fence.

"Get it, Cartboy!" shouted Ryan. "He's running home."

I hopped the fence into the neighbor's yard. And that's when I got my first look at Wolfie.

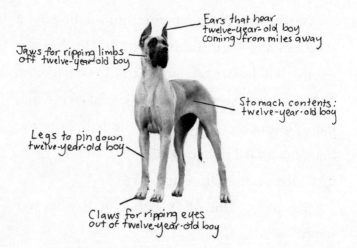

Ears that hear twelve-year-old boy coming from miles away

Jaws for ripping limbs off twelve-year-old boy

Stomach contents: twelve-year-old boy

Legs to pin down twelve-year-old boy

Claws for ripping eyes out of twelve-year-old boy

"Nice, Wolfie. Good boy," I whispered, trying to get close to the ball.

"Grrrrr!"

"Good boy. Everything's okay."

"*Rowwwf!*"

Suddenly, Wolfie opened his massive jaw and *lunged* at me. I grabbed the ball and made it back over the fence just as the rabid beast took a chunk out of my shoe.

"I quit," I said.

"You mean you don't want your turn hitting?" Garth held up a shiny new bat. "Just one more out and you're up."

I had to admit, that bat did look good. I was dying to do some hitting.

"All right. But I'm not going over that fence again."

Garth was up at bat next. The first pitch came and he swung hard. *Strike!* He missed. The second pitch came, he swung, and *crack*!

A line drive right over the fence.

"Get it, Cartboy! Go!"

This time, I didn't need to hop over the fence. Because Ryan picked me up and *tossed* me over.

I tried to get back over the fence, but halfway up I got stuck. I fell back into Wolfie's pen and waited to die. I probably would have if Arnie hadn't come to help me. He distracted Wolfie with a baseball, and I managed to make it out of there with my pants and one shoe. I don't know what happened to my shirt. I think Wolfie swallowed it.

Arnie and I ran all the way to my house without looking back once. We burst through the door and into the kitchen, where my mom was feeding the twins.

"Hal, your clothes are ripped to shreds! What have you been doing?"

What could I say?

"Sports."

Before my mom could say anything else,

Arnie and I ran into the tiny room I share with the twins.

"Man, that Ryan Horner is a creep," I said as I grabbed some new clothes. "Seriously, we are never trusting him again."

"Never," said Arnie. "Are you okay?"

"I'm pretty sure I need to change my underwear. But otherwise, I'm fine. Thanks for the rescue, Arn."

Arnie and I decided to go into my tiny backyard and play catch by ourselves. But first, we gave each other a manpat. It's this high-five/backslap/fist-pound combo we invented to show each other some support.

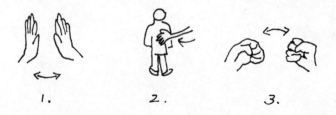

1.   2.   3.

I might not have many friends, but I'm lucky I have a good one.

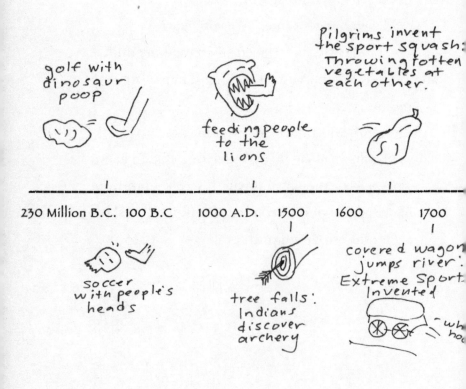

golf with
dinosaur
poop

feeding people
to the
lions

Pilgrims invent
the sport squash:
Throwing rotten
vegetables at
each other.

230 Million B.C.   100 B.C   1000 A.D.   1500   1600   1700

soccer
with people's
heads

tree falls:
Indians
discover
archery

covered wagon
jumps river:
Extreme Sport
Invented

-wh
hoo

football
invented:
small Kids
everywhere
become
less
popular

pizza chef
tosses dough
to dog:
The Birth of
Frisbee

|———————————————|——————————————|——————————|————————————————

1800   1900   1960   The Future

man + log +
avalanche =
snowboarding

molecularly
modified
shape-shifting
ball

Fame

Dear ?

These days, getting famous is pretty easy. Everybody has a chance. All you need is a camera and an idea. It could be weird or cute or smart or dangerous. Or just plain dumb. As long as something about your idea makes people want to watch it. And send it to their friends.

Thanks to something called YouTube, they can.

Cindy Shano taped her dog "singing" "Happy Birthday."
It got ten million views.

It doesn't hurt that everyone can watch You-Tube on their cell phones too. Practically every time I look at Arnie, he's watching something on his phone. It's his favorite thing in the world, especially since he got a custom purple plaid case. If you asked Arnie to give up his leg or his phone, he'd probably go with the leg.

With all this fame everywhere, it's hard to resist the temptation to get in on the action. Even though I can't act or sing, and shake like Jell-O when I even get near a stage, I let Arnie convince me to try out for the fall play.

"C'mon, Hal," Arnie said. "The whole school will be watching. You'll be able to get any girl you want to go to the middle school dance with you after this."

What Arnie can never seem to remember is that I have *no plans* to go to the middle school dance. I am *never* going to the middle school dance. I've told him this a thousand times. I'd rather be trapped in a meat locker with the Wedgiemeister than go to the middle school dance.

"Besides," said Arnie, "Mr. Tupkin is directing it this year."

I didn't have to think it over for long to realize trying out for the school play might not be such a bad idea after all. If I did land a role, two things could happen.

1. I'd get on Mr. Tupkin's good side.
2. My mom would be so impressed, I

would be able to negotiate extra video-game time. Maybe, if I got the lead, she'd up me to twenty-five whole minutes on the weekends.

MINUTES CURRENTLY ALLOWED
TO PLAY RAVENCAVE:
15
MINUTES IT TAKES TO POWER UP SYSTEM:
6
MINUTES OF REAL PLAYING TIME:
9

The play was *The Wind in the Willows,* and open auditions were one Friday after school. I don't know if you and your classmates or alien buddies are still performing this play in the future, but right now, it's considered a "timeless classic."

As far as I can tell, it's about a bunch of rodents who talk like the Queen of England.

There was only one good role—the fine, good-natured Mole.

Mole had morals, dignity, grace, and a costume that didn't crush your kiwis. He dared to leave the underground for the sake of adventure and some fresh air.

A real mole.
I am not sure if this is the back or the front.

Of course, Arnie and I both wanted to be Mole badly. Arnie to get girls, both of us to reach Level 13.

Arnie's parents are pretty stingy with the video-game playing too, so no matter whose house we're at, our RavenCave time is limited. The fact that his mom and my mom are best friends doesn't help either. They sit around drinking coffee and talking about how video games "corrupt a boy's brain."

I thought I had a decent shot at the role of Mole. I have small ears, brown hair, and when I'm watching wrestling on television, I like to burrow under my Snuggie. (It's a blanket that's all the rage right now. It has sleeves. Yep, sleeves.)

It turned out Ryan Horner wanted the role of Mole even worse than Arnie or me. And it was pretty obvious why. Ryan was dying to ask Jamie Levitt to the dance, and she just loves the sensitive actor types.

Only one thing was for sure: auditions would be a clawing, gnawing rat fight to the death.

Arnie and I started rehearsing, memorizing Mole's lines, trying to get the edge. We figured we would much rather see one of us get to be Mole than Ryan Horner.

But way before the audition, Ryan suddenly started acting extremely *moley*, especially when Mr. Tupkin was around.

Other kids couldn't tell, but Arnie and I spotted Ryan's cheating ways a mile away: eating a burger in the cafeteria by nibbling tiny circular bites all the way around. Wearing a fur vest, "because he was chilly." Constantly digging for stuff in his locker.

"I know what you're up to," I said to Ryan.

"I have no idea what you're talking about, Cartboy," he said, rubbing some dirt on his nose.

"Knock it off, this isn't fair. You're trying to steal the lead," said Arnie.

But Ryan was way too busy opening a jar of worms and grubs and showing it to every kid in the hallway.

Ryan's extreme moliness worked like a charm on Mr. Tupkin. He had pretty much made up his mind long before the auditions, and it was all over before it began.

Ryan got to be Mole. Arnie and I got the roles of Stoat One and Stoat Two.

Stoat: a small member of the weasel family that no one has ever seen.

On opening night, I stood backstage while my knees were practically knocking together. Sweat ran down my stoat hair, over my stoat forehead, and into my stoat eyes.

Arnie gave me a nudge. "Here's our cue, Hal. Let's go."

"I can't do it."

"Everyone's waiting. C'mon."

"I have wet fur in my eyes. . . ."

"All you have to do is get out there and say

one line. 'What happened to the houseboat?' It'll be over in a second."

I tried to wipe the sopping hair off my face, to get some visibility going, but all that did was rub *more* fur off my paws and into my eyes. The audience was fidgeting, and all the while, Mr. Tupkin was staring at me the same way he does in history class.

A couple of people coughed, and I heard someone behind me say, "Get going, Cartboy."

That's when I felt the paw on my back. Not just any paw. A thick, puffy, moley paw. A paw that could only belong to Ryan Horner.

Ryan gave me a hard shove toward the cardboard riverbank near the edge of the stage. Suddenly, I was under the hot lights sweating even more.

I turned to Arnie, and, giving it my deepest, stoatiest voice, asked, "What happened to the . . ."

The last word had somehow disappeared from my brain, so I cleared my throat and tried again. "What happened to the . . . to the . . ."

I searched around the stage for a clue as to what I was supposed to say. Every second that went by felt like *an hour.*

I guess all that silence was a cue for Ryan Horner to spring back into action. And give me *another* hard shove. I'd like to think that when he pushed me again, he was trying to be helpful. To jog my memory. But knowing Ryan Horner, I'd say he was taking the opportunity to act like a jerk.

The second shove was even harder than the first. And the next thing I remember, I was on the trombone player Terry Smit's lap.

Of course everyone in the audience was taping the whole thing. When they got home, lots of them decided to post their videos (send them over to YouTube), so the whole world could see them too.

I guess a five-foot stoat doing a flip off a stage is the kind of thing people like to watch. A lot. I got to discover firsthand what it's like to "go viral."

Sometimes it's hard being famous. Like, even if I'm just going out to play some handball in the park, a stranger will recognize me, and yell, "What happened to the!"

But you learn to cope.

monkey swings
from tree

monkey raids
king tut's
tomb

2 million years ago   50,000 years ago   1200 BC   1780

monkey dances
on rock

monkey pe
on George
Washington
Cherry tree

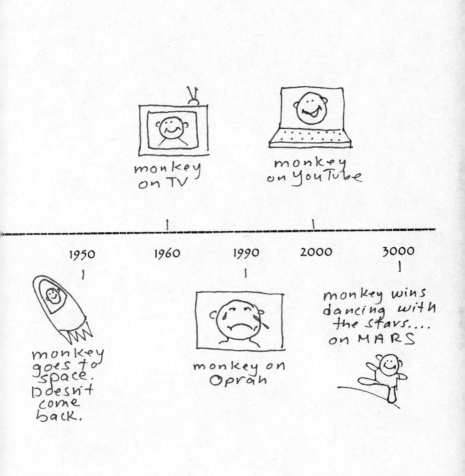

monkey
on TV

monkey
on YouTube

1950 1960 1990 2000 3000

monkey
goes to
space.
Doesn't
come
back.

monkey on
Oprah

monkey wins
dancing with
the stars....
on MARS

The Information Age

Dear (fill in your name here):

They call the era I live in the Information Age.

This is because if you do something embarrassing, even worse than falling off the stage in the school play, the entire school will know about it in four minutes. That was how long it took everyone to find out what happened in the cafeteria today.

Today's popular gossip-transmitting devices.

It all started when I was standing on the lunch line trying to decide what to eat. It was between the rib-b-que on a bun and the beefy nachos, and I was having a lot of trouble choosing. The main reason being that today was "Simm's Surprise Day." It's the one time every month when Mr. Simms, the cafeteria manager, gets to pick whatever he wants to serve. All on the spur of the moment. Unfortunately what he usually wants to serve is the stuff that's about to expire in the back of the fridge, and the "surprise" is a hunk of mold in your cheeseburger.

My eyes went back and forth between the bun and the nachos, the bun and the nachos.

"Hurry up, Cartboy," shouted Ryan Horner from the end of the line.

"I'll have the uh . . . um . . . uhhh . . ." I said to the lady behind the counter.

Suddenly, my stomach did what felt like a backflip with a twist. But this was much more than the usual barfy feeling I get on Simm's Surprise Day. It was a deep, low growwwwl.

"I'll take the rib . . . I mean the beef . . . I mean, wait . . ."

Growwwwl.

The next backflip came with a churning

noise that could be heard from three tables away. Both Cindy Shano and Hilary Valentine looked up.

"You better not let one blow, Cartboy," said Cindy, baring her fangs and braces.

Growwwwl.

Which brings me to the other reason I couldn't choose a lunch, and it had nothing to do with Simm's Surprise. It was because my stomach was starting to pay for what I had eaten at Arnie's house last night.

Both of Arnie's parents were at work, and guess who they asked to watch Arnie and me? None other than Garth and Ryan Horner.

Garth and Ryan would rather see Arnie and me get mauled by bobcats than provide any actual childcare. So when we told them we were hungry, they said there were microwavable burritos in the freezer and to go "get them yourselves, dipwads."

We dug out the burritos from underneath some pie crusts that Arnie's mom had made back in the nineties, scraped off the white glacial coating, and popped them in the microwave on high.

Burrito.

The kind of thing you get when you Google "burrito."

I figured those burritos were kind of dicey. But my feet grew three sizes last year, and when I need to eat, I need to eat. I had to chew nine times the normal amount and I'm pretty sure I chipped my left molar, but eventually, I choked it down.

I guess it can take a food item with that much freezer burn a while to make its way through the digestive system. So it was about fourteen hours later in health and wellness when the dam broke.

What started out as a series of small growls quickly turned into a deafening rumble that could only be caused by one thing. A gigantic gas bubble with one place to go.

Out.

I tried squeezing my cheeks together, to keep the monster inside, but unfortunately, squeezing had an effect similar to letting air out of an over-blown balloon.

PFFFFFFFT!!

Thirty seconds later the bell rang and you never saw a bunch of crazed kids grab their phones faster. What's nice about the Information Age is that not only do the devices exist for trans-mitting instant information, there are all kinds of shortcuts and abbreviations for words.

WHT'S THT SML?

HAL CUT 1

HAL + BUTT = KBOOM!

As I walked to my locker with Arnie, there wasn't a person in the hall who didn't hold their nose and wave their hand in front of their face.

"This does not help your date prospects for the middle school dance," Arnie said.

"Which, as I told you four million times, I am not going to. . . ."

But Arnie wasn't paying much attention. He was busy looking across the hall at Heather Fukumoto, the girl he wanted to ask to the dance.

Arnie decided to go talk to Heather, so he put his phone down in his locker. He didn't hear it beep again. But I did. And I couldn't help but pick it up and read it.

STAY UPWIND FRM CARTBOY
IF U KNOW WHT I MEAN

The weirdest thing wasn't the text itself. It was that the text was from *Ryan Horner*.

And there was more.

MEET 2 TALK ABT SECRET

How did Ryan get Arnie's number? We hate Ryan. We had a pact to never talk to him again. And besides that, what secret? The only secret Arnie and I cared about was where Susie was hiding the scythe. Arnie wouldn't get that from Ryan behind my back.

Would he?

Human Communicatio

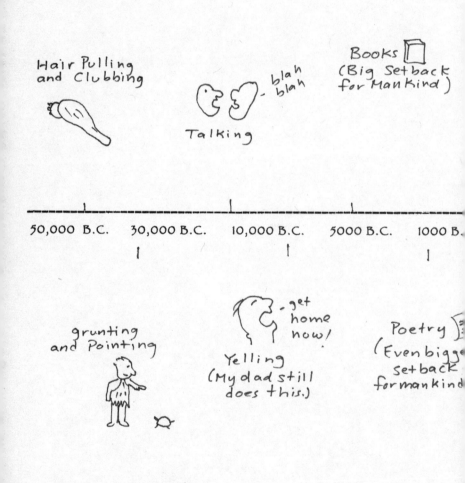

Hair Pulling
and Clubbing

blah
blah

Talking

Books
(Big Setback
for Mankind)

50,000 B.C.   30,000 B.C.   10,000 B.C.   5000 B.C.   1000 B.

grunting
and Pointing

- get
home
now!

Yelling
(My dad still
does this.)

Poetry
(Even bigg
setback
for mankind

hrough the Ages

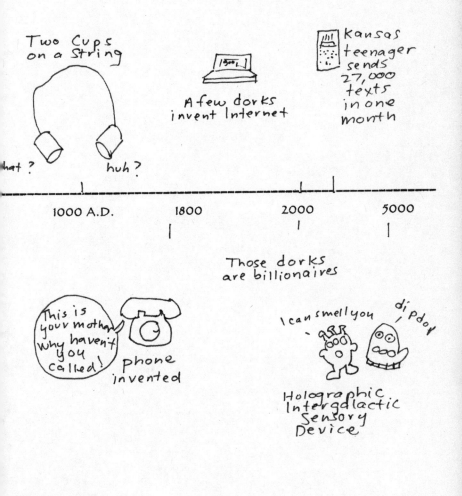

Dating

Dear Future Wanderer of the Earth:

Arnie isn't the only person in Stowfield who's obsessed with whether or not I'm going to the middle school dance. Even though it's only the beginning of December, and the dance isn't until February, almost *three months* away, my mom is all up in a tizzy about it too.

The other day, she was sitting in the kitchen changing Bea and Perrie's diapers. "So who are you taking to the dance, Hal?" she asked as she threw a full diaper into the trash.

"I'm not going to the dance, Mom."

"Why don't you ask a nice girl, like Cindy Shano? You two could double-date with Arnie!"

Like all the other parents in Stowfield, my mom thinks Cindy Shano is the nicest kid ever because she gets good grades, sucks up to the teachers, and made a famous video about her dog. As if that's not bad enough, just the mention of Arnie made me think of that text he got from Ryan Horner. The idea that Arnie and Ryan might have a secret together sent a shiver down my back.

My mom must've seen a weird expression come across my face because right away she said, "What's the matter, honey?"

Before I could answer, she stood up and shouted in the direction of the spare room where my dad was fixing a lawn mower.

"Family powwow!"

"Family powwow" is the thing my mom shouts out every time she thinks there's an issue we need to discuss. She says powwows are in the spirit of good communication and that they help our family build "mutual respect and a strong bond." Or something like that. Every week, we have to gather in a circle "just like the Native Americans did" and have "an open exchange of feelings and ideas."

Does this man look like he wants
to talk about feelings?

Mom takes family powwow very seriously and sometimes they go on for like, an hour. Even Bea and Perrie have learned to recognize the word *powwow.* Whenever they hear it, they both crawl over to me and climb on my legs like they're hoping I'll run out of the room and take them with me.

"Mom, it's okay, we don't need to have a powwow . . ." I started to say, but didn't get too far.

My dad immediately appeared in the kitchen doorway. "I'm all ears!"

"Martin, explain to Hal that being attracted to girls in sixth grade is perfectly normal and nothing to be ashamed of." My mom turned from my dad to me. "Hal, when Dad was your age he was dating Charlene Denton. She was a ballerina!"

My dad had a grease mark stretching from his ear to his shoulder, and it was pretty hard to see why Charlene Denton or anyone else would go on a date with him.

"Son," he said in the serious voice he usually saves for history quotes. "When a boy begins to travel down the special highway that leads to manhood, he will experience many confusing changes. Sudden cravings and desires. Nervousness about dating girls. Hair in the armpits." He put his hand on my shoulder. "Who better to guide that boy through those changes than his father?"

I hoped Mom might step in to save me, but instead she said, "I think it's time you two discussed the facts of life."

The only thing worse than family powwow, or carrying an old-lady cart to school, is a talk with your dad about "the facts of life."

If you ever come across a book like this,
run for your life.

"Don't be shy, Hal. It's all perfectly natural," said my mom.

I needed to bolt out of the kitchen immediately, but my dad was blocking the door. I slumped down in a kitchen chair and a thought came to me. Maybe, for once, it was time to put the family powwow to good use.

"Well, since you mentioned dating, Mom, there actually is one girl I'm thinking of."

My mom practically jumped out of her skin. "Who is it? Who is she? Do we know her? God, I love family powwow."

The truth is, I actually *was* thinking of a girl. But it wasn't Cindy Shano. I mean, sure, Cindy isn't always completely annoying, and she does have a vintage Metallica T-shirt that I am completely jealous of. But the girl I was thinking of at that moment was Susie on RavenCave. It's been really gnawing at me that Arnie and I *still* haven't gotten her to find the scythe.

Unless, of course, Arnie doesn't care about RavenCave anymore. Since he's been getting *secret texts* from Ryan Horner.

"Mom," I said, "you were right. The girl I'm thinking of is Cindy Shano."

Perrie let out a little yelp. My mom did too.

"But, the thing is, I would like to get to know her a little better. You know, to see if I want to ask her to the dance. And that's just so hard to do when I don't have my own room."

Okay, I know it sounded like a long shot. But seeing as how badly my mom wanted me to go to the dance with Cindy, I had to try it. All I needed to do was convince my mom that having my own room was the best way to get alone time with Cindy Shano. Sure, once I got my own room, I'd pretty much just play RavenCave, but that was a minor detail my parents didn't need to know.

I noticed that as soon as I put the idea out there, my dad stiffened up. It was like he knew I was trying to wiggle around my history grade to get the spare room. But one look at my mom and he softened up.

"Well, son, I suppose if I had a shed for my

appliance parts in the backyard, I could give up the extra room."

I could tell from the way my dad was talking, I was the one who would have to build most of the shed. Even if Arnie helped me it would probably take like, five weekends, and we'd have to make it out of scrap wood from the dump. But I didn't want to think about that now. The shed seemed like the best chance I had.

Just add 9,473 nails.

The next day at school I was feeling pretty pumped. That is until I ran into Arnie. He was talking to Ryan in the hallway, but as soon as they saw me Ryan walked away.

"What were you talking to Ryan about?"

Arnie pretended he didn't hear me.

"So you like Cindy Shano?" he said. "Not an obvious choice, with the braces and the constant put-downs and making fun of you behind your back." Arnie grabbed a science book from his locker. "You going to ask her to the dance?"

I hadn't figured on the fact that my mom talks to Arnie's mom practically every day. She probably called her with the "big news" the second I left the room.

"No, I'm not going to ask her to the dance. Because I'm *not going to the dance.* Anyway, what were you and Ryan talking about?"

"Nothing."

The bell rang and before I could ask Arnie any more questions, he practically skipped down the hallway.

"We could double-date," he said over his shoulder. "I'm going with Heather Fukumoto."

I turned the other way and headed toward

history class. As I walked down the hallway, I couldn't help but wish I lived in the future.

Either that or in the way-distant past. Like medieval times. Or dinosaur times. Or any times before dating existed.

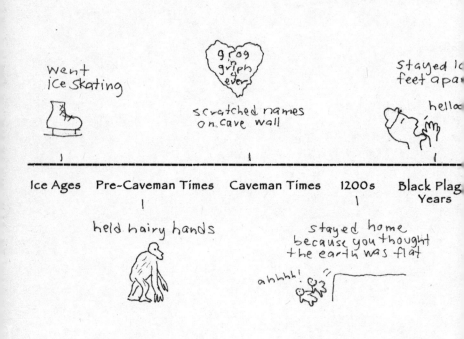

Went ice skating

grog 'n griph 4 ever

scratched names on cave wall

stayed l[c] feet apa[r]

hell[o]

| Ice Ages | Pre-Caveman Times | Caveman Times | 1200s | Black Plag[ue] Years |

held hairy hands

stayed home because you thought the earth was flat

ahhhh!

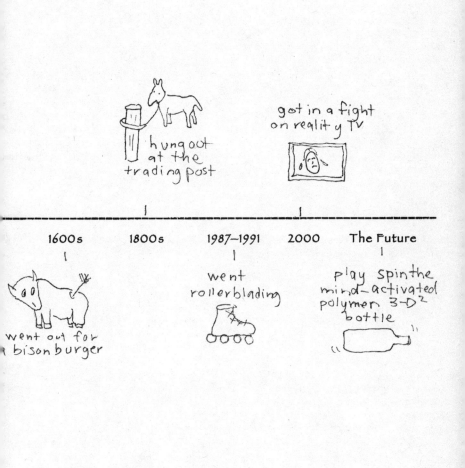

hung out
at the
trading post

got in a fight
on reality TV

1600s   1800s   1987–1991   2000   The Future

went out for
a bison burger

went
rollerblading

play spin the
mind-activated
polymer $3\text{-}D^2$
bottle

Food

Dear, Um, Whoever You Are:

Mr. Tupkin was telling us that since the beginning of time, people have needed one fundamental thing to survive. "Be sure to write about food for the time capsule. I'm sure your future reader would be quite interested in knowing the culinary tastes and innovations of the early twenty-first century."

The first thing I thought when Mr. Tupkin mentioned food was, Who cares! Who needs it when your dad is going to kill you anyway?

It turns out I got a D- on the midterm test.

Mr. Tupkin gave it to us the *first day* after Christmas break. I know I should have done better, but this one was a first-class colonial brain bender. Loyalists, Founding Fathers, rebels, patriots, minutemen. You get the idea.

This time, it wasn't enough for Mr. Tupkin to send me home with an extra forty pounds of books. He also had to write a letter to my parents, complete with one of his "deep" quotes.

Dear Mr. and Mrs. Rifkind—
Hal must improve his study habits or he will not receive a passing grade.
"That men do not learn very much from the lessons of history is the most important of all the lessons that history has to teach."
—Mr. Tupkin

Never mind that I'm good at handball and know everything about the Ziptuk E300S. That

I'm a serious competitor on RavenCave and got to Level 3 in seven weeks. My parents didn't want to hear about any of those accomplishments.

My dad barged into the room I share with Bea and Perrie and read Mr. Tupkin's letter out loud.

"Hal. How many times have I told you? History is the self-consciousness of humanity. If you want to understand today, you must search yesterday."

"Um. Uh-huh."

"George Washington was one of the bravest men our country has ever had. Do you know why?"

"He agreed to appear on the dollar bill in a wig that makes him look like Gramma?"

"No. George Washington had character. The only way to inspire other people is to be a good person yourself."

"Dad, you and Mr. Tupkin say a lot of complicated quotes. I'm not exactly sure what they mean."

"How about this for clarity. You can forget about having your own room until I see at *least* a B on your next report card."

Clearly, I needed to figure out a way to get on my dad's good side without having to study history.

Luckily, during family powwow this week, my mom gave me a chance. And it had to do with food.

"Hal, I don't want to make you frightened or anything, but over the years I've allowed your body to become a toxic waste dump. It's too late to do anything to save you."

Just as I was trying to digest this thought, she said, "Thank God there's still time to salvage the twins. From now on, we're going to eat local."

I couldn't believe my luck because we have a Dunkin' Donuts three blocks away, and what could be more local than that?

Sadly, that wasn't the point. Local means eating vegetables and stuff that are grown near you so you don't waste gas getting them to the store.

Before I even had a chance to make myself a final "H.R." burger (a quarter-pound bacon cheeseburger with two chocolate-glazed doughnuts in place of the buns), everything in our house changed.

fat — fat
sugar — greasy fat

All meat was replaced with tofu. Eggs were gone. And "cheese" became some sort of rice product that only tasted like cheese if you held your nose when you ate it.

"Why stop at local when you can go vegan!" said my mom, who started wearing hemp sweat-shirts and shoes made out of hay.

"Mom, we can't go vegan," I said. "If the lack of meat and dairy doesn't kill us, the withdrawal symptoms will."

"You'll get used to it. And one day, you'll thank me."

Believe it or not, this whole vegan thing hit my dad even harder than me. He was raised on a farm in Poland and grew up on kielbasa (a kind of hot dog), bratwurst (a kind of hot dog), and hot dogs. I'm pretty sure they grind up meat and put it in baby bottles over there.

Mmm...pork chops...

My mom's new rule of "no meat ever" quickly started to make my dad depressed. I'd never seen a man so down in the dumps. The truth was, I was having a tough time too.

Last week, on the way back from Grampa Janson's house, we pulled over at the Rawhide Steakhouse on Route 17 just to breathe in the fumes from the grill. We even hung out in the parking lot of a Burger Barn hoping to sniff some airborne molecules of flame-broiled beef.

Things were rough, but slowly my dad and I made progress. We learned some good tricks. Like, if you put a whole bottle of ketchup on a tofu burger, it's not half bad. Or, with enough soy milk, you can choke down a gluten-free doughnut.

All this healthy eating meant my dad and I finally had something in common. The other day, when my mom asked the two of us to watch the twins while she went shopping with Aunt Trudy, we sat up straight as arrows.

"You bet!" said my dad.

Right away, I could tell what my dad was thinking. 'Cause I was thinking the exact same thing.

When it comes to babysitting, my dad and I are both pretty horrible at it. We usually catch one of the girls falling off the coffee table or pulling a quarter out of her mouth. Stuff that never happens when my mom is around. And forget dressing them to go outside. It takes us about three hours to get ready for a five-minute walk in the park.

But the second my mom pulled out of the driveway, you never saw two people get a pair of toddlers in a double stroller faster. Three minutes. We headed into town at about seventy miles an hour, a seriously fuel-wasting speed for my dad.

"Mr. Rifkind! Hal! Haven't seen either of you in a while," said the butcher, Mr. Hahn.

My dad, being my dad, quickly scanned the meat to see what was on sale. He wasn't about to actually pay real money for something, even though he wanted it bad. He offered to repair Mr. Hahn's cold-cut slicer in exchange for two steaks, four pork chops, and a pound of bacon. Mr. Hahn agreed, and started to wrap up the meat.

"Make it fast," said my dad. "And remember, you never saw us."

While a confused Mr. Hahn put the meat in brown paper, my dad and I pressed our noses against the glass butcher case, eyeing the chops and sausages like a couple of jailbirds looking at freedom.

By the time we made it to the sidewalk, my dad was wondering if we could actually eat the steaks raw. "They call it steak tartare in the fancy restaurants," he said, wrapping his hands around a bloody rib eye and raising it to his lips.

III

I was like, "Dad, that can't be good for you. . . ." But by the time we got to the car, I too had not just licked, but gnawed off a corner of the steak.

The minute we got home, we fired up the barbecue. It didn't even cross our minds that it was January in Pennsylvania and the temperature was way below freezing. There was enough food for a soccer team and we were going to grill it. Our meatfest included no girly utensils, no wussy plates. Just our hands, mouths, and incisors.

Recipe

grilled Steak

1. Fire up the grill*
2. Toss on the steak

*If you are an advanced ape who can read and has hairy arms, I recommend oven mitts!

About halfway through our carnivore-athon, just as I was giving my dad a high five, my mom called to say she was on her way home. It gave us just enough time to cover the evidence. We used rubber gloves and bleach, just like they do on my dad's favorite show, *Law & Order*.

We scraped the last bit of gristle off the barbecue just in time to see my mom get out of the car lugging her reusable tote bags filled with stuff from the green market.

She walked in the backyard and immediately started sniffing the air. "Something's not right. What's going on here?"

"Just cleaning up," my dad said, licking a chunk of beef off his tooth. "We made cumin-rubbed tofu."

"On the barbecue? It's twelve degrees outside!"

"But, Mom, grilled tofu is the best. So flavorful," I added casually as I removed the pink rubber gloves.

"Interesting that you two cleaned the grill so thoroughly . . ."

"When it comes to barbecues, you can't be too neat," I said. "Keeps the raccoons away."

My mom glared at the rubber gloves and the bleach bottle near the bottom of the grill. "In the kitchen. Now, Hal."

I ditched the gloves and followed her to the kitchen. My heart was beating fast. I had a feeling this was not going to be pretty, especially when she pulled out a dining chair next to Perrie and made me sit down.

"Cumin-rubbed tofu? You expect me to believe that, Hal?"

Perrie pulled a bacon strip out of her dress and waved it around like a flag.

"Okay, maybe we seasoned it with a *little* pork."

"I knew it!"

"But it was hardly anything. Really, Mom. One little piece of bacon," I said.

Perrie held up her fingers. "Twee!"

"Okay, three. But we were desperate. I thought Dad was going to start eating the leather chair in the living room."

Makes a good soup
if you're hungry enough.

"Dad cooking meat, I can understand," said my mom. "He was raised eating pigs' knuckles for breakfast. But you. You should know better. You of all people should be following the rules of this house. And to think I've been telling your dad to give you your own room, even though Mr. Tupkin said your history grade is barely a D!"

I yanked the bacon out of Perrie's hand and threw it in the trash. "Mom, it'll never happen again."

She stormed out of the kitchen, leaving me alone with Perrie, who started digging around in the trash for the bacon.

"I promise I'll bring up my grade," I shouted at the kitchen door. But she was off to unload her beans and brown rice from the car.

I couldn't help but wonder what Mom would have done if she knew the whole truth. That besides the bacon, there were steaks and pork chops too. If she did know the truth, she would have grounded me on the spot and I probably wouldn't get my own room until I was eighteen.

I know this sounds crazy, but I swear sometimes I catch the twins looking at me as if they know *exactly* what Dad and I did. They say babies are a lot smarter than they look, and just because they can't talk that much doesn't mean they don't understand. Sometimes my dad and I get a little creeped out when the girls stare at us. Like they would tell Mom the whole story if they could.

In the meantime, I figure it can't hurt to play it safe. When we're at the grocery store, I make it a point to hold up a giant leg of lamb for the twins, point at it, and say, "tofu."

The Thing

anything you could outrun

bark

Anything you could grow

anything you could steal

anything you could eat with r teeth

80,000 years ago   5,000 B.C.   2,000 B.C.   1000 B.C

eople Eat

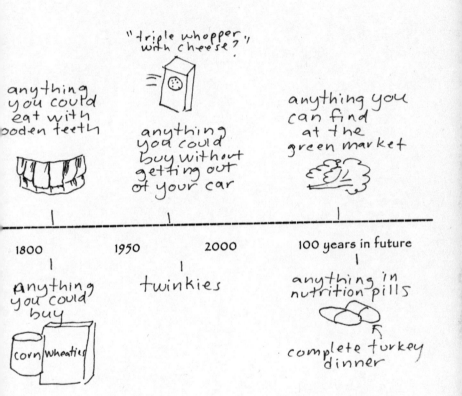

"triple whopper with cheese?"

anything you could eat with wooden teeth

anything you could buy without getting out of your car

anything you can find at the green market

1800   1950   2000   100 years in future

anything you could buy

corn | wheaties

twinkies

anything in nutrition pills

complete turkey dinner

Clothing

Dear Future Being Whose Name I Don't Know:

A few days ago when I was getting dressed for school, my mom walked into my room and put a crumpled bag on my bed.

"Here, Hal, I got you some new clothes."

That's what my mom always says when she gives me a bag of hand-me-downs, which are about all I wear.

"Thanks, Mom. When you say new, do you mean *new*, like you went to the mall and bought me something that fits? Or *new*, as in they once belonged to Garth, he wore them to shreds, and now they're mine."

"Oh, Hal. What's the difference?"

Arnie refuses to wear Garth's hand-me-downs, but my mom gladly takes them. Once again, because it's "green."

If you ever saw a pair of Garth's jeans on me, you'd give me an award for helping save Planet Earth. They are about three sizes too big, and the cut is called husky. I could fit a sack of potatoes between me and a pair of slim-cut jeans, so you can imagine what it takes to get Garth's pants to stay above my knees.

Ropes, suspenders, glue guns, you name it, I've tried it.

Sasquatch: one of the few creatures on Earth who is bigger than Garth.

"Mom, no one loves old Planet Earth more than me. But, what do you say, just this once, we get me some new pants that cover my underwear in gym class."

"Hal Rifkind. You know as well as I do that brand-new clothing is a needless frivolity. Look at me, I'm wearing Aunt Trudy's garden shoes."

She held up an orange clog and a small chunk of manure fell to the kitchen floor.

My mom started to walk away, and I glanced down at the bag of clothes on the table. A gnarly brown soda stain on Garth's T-shirt seemed to stare right back at me. I could swear the stain had a face with two beady little eyes and growling lips, just like Garth. Before I knew what was happening, my mouth suddenly flew open.

"Mom. I need to look good at the middle school dance on Friday."

What possessed me to say that? I have no plans to go to the middle school dance. Ever. Sure, back in November I mentioned I was thinking of taking Cindy Shano, but I never actually *meant* it.

If you see one of these T-shirts someplace, it probably belonged to garth.

"The gym Special"   "who barfed?"   "Ahh-chooo!"

My mom stopped in her tracks. A shriek flew out of her mouth that sounded like half car alarm, half eight-year-old girl.

"Oh my God! You're really going to the middle school dance! Cindy said yes! She is sooo cute in the doggie video! Are you going to kiss her? I *have* to chaperone. I'll bring a camera. Oh, I need to get that on film!"

My mom ran off, probably to call Arnie's mom, Cindy's mom, and every other mom in town. I just stood there in the middle of the kitchen, in the deep grave I'd just dug for myself.

I had no idea what to do. The dance was on Friday, just days away! How did February get here so fast? All I knew was I had to go to school and Cindy Shano would be there for sure.

The next day, I walked up to my locker pulling my squeaky cart, my clothes hanging off me like some sort of denim parachute. I didn't even unpack my books. Instead, I just opened my locker and stared at the deep mess inside.

"What's the matter with you?"

Arnie's locker is next to mine, and he was just about the last person I wanted to see.

"What's happening, Hal?"

I tried to ignore Arnie, mainly because I caught him talking to Ryan Horner *again* yesterday. This time, they were outside the cafeteria. The second they saw me, they split up.

But once Arnie saw the expression on my face, he wouldn't leave me alone.

"I can tell something's wrong, Hal."

I must have been desperate because I ended up telling Arnie everything that happened. That I told my mom I was going to the dance because I wanted new clothes. That she thought I already asked Cindy Shano, but that really I hadn't.

"Well, you have to ask Cindy to the dance now," said Arnie. "I'm sure your mom has talked to her mom. It's probably a done deal."

"I wouldn't say done—"

"Heather and I will pick up you and Cindy on the way. Trust me, this is going to be good."

"It's not going to be good. Because it's not going to happen. . . ."

But Arnie wasn't listening. And when I turned

around, I could see why. Cindy Shano was standing at the end of the hallway.

"There she is now, Hal." Arnie gave me a nudge. "Go ahead. Ask her. Hurry, the bell's going to ring."

My talk with Arnie would have to wait. Between my mom, Arnie, and the size forty-two pants bunching up at my ankles, I knew I would have to ask Cindy right away.

I stood up fast, but my giant jeans got wedged in the cart and I couldn't get them free. "Garth's pants, I mean my pants, I mean *the pants I'm wearing* are stuck on the cart."

"Just go!"

I tore my pants free, and squeaked down the hallway toward Cindy.

Squeak.

"Hey, Cindy."

Squeak.

"What do you want, Cartboy?"

"Nice to see you too. I wanted to . . ."

Squeak.

". . . ask you a question."

Cindy looked at me and curled her face up as if she was smelling something bad, which, given the yellow armpit stains on Garth's T-shirt, she probably was.

I tried to see past the purple braces and the snarl. I tried to forget about the way she and her friends laugh at me in history class. Surely there was a kind person in there somewhere.

"Do you want to . . . go . . . to . . . the . . . ahh . . ."

She sucked a small gob of spit out of her braces. "Do I want to what?"

"Do you want to go . . . to . . . the . . . ahh . . . the, ahh . . . history. Do you want to tutor me in history class?"

Not only had I completely chickened out, and not only would I not be getting any new clothes,

I had also just possibly made myself have to study history with Cindy Shano.

"Two conditions," she said. "One, you pay me. Two, you supply the food. I like taffy, beef jerky, and Milk Duds. Half an hour, your house. Once."

I wonder if Cindy has the same
number of teeth as George Washington.

That afternoon, when she showed up at my house, the truth was, I was kind of relieved. Yes, this tutoring thing would be torture. Yes, I wished I was playing RavenCave. But if I studied with Cindy, I might actually pass history.

The second Cindy and I walked through the kitchen door, my mom ran up to us. "Helloooo, Cindy. Sooo nice to see you! Well, why don't I leave you two alone. . . ."

I felt my face turn bright red. "Where should we start, Cindy?" I asked. "Valley Forge? The Boston Tea Party?"

But instead of cracking a book, all Cindy did was send about a million texts. Her fingers were moving so fast I could barely see them. All the while she was texting, she kept muttering to herself.

"Jerk! I can't believe it. She did not! With him? He was supposed to ask me!"

Before I knew it, Cindy was crying and I had to give her like, fifteen tissues just to stop the waterworks. I could only make out about one of every six words, but she seemed to be saying something about having no date, looking like a fool, never going alone . . .

Suddenly Cindy put down her phone and looked up at me. "Hal, I really can't stand to be within three feet of you, I think you are really dumb, and I'd rather wade through elephant diarrhea than be seen with you, but . . . will you go to the dance with me?"

"Well, when you put it like that, Cindy . . ."

"I've been humiliated by Scott Baer. He was supposed to ask me, but he asked Darby Hoenicker, that little twerp, and now I have no one. Please. I'll give you free tutoring. You can have the Milk Duds."

She looked up at me with big watery eyes, her top lip caught on her braces.

"You don't have to worry about the tutoring, Cindy. And you can keep the Milk Duds. I'll take you."

Cindy looked relieved and a little bit scared. I was pretty scared too, especially because Friday, the day of the dance, came up pretty quick.

Right after school, my mom took me to the mall for new clothes. I discovered a special little world that I never knew existed. It's called the three-mirror dressing room. You get to try stuff on to see if it looks good from a million different angles. I got a bunch of things, like new sneakers, a new pair of jeans, and a special shirt. Lots of kids said they were getting dressed up, so I figured I better too.

The tuxedo T-shirt:
fools 'em every time.

That night, Arnie and I picked up Heather and Cindy and walked over to school, with *our moms* following us the whole way. Even though the walk was just two miles, it felt like a thousand. I kept trying to think of something to say to Cindy. At one point, I asked her if her dog sang anything besides "Happy Birthday," but she just glared at me and kept quiet.

When we got to the dance, I had no plans to hang out with Cindy Shano or do dancing of any kind. But then something came over me. I'm not sure what it was. Maybe the clothes from the mall. Maybe the feeling of wearing underpants that I was the first to own. I felt like a new man.

The song "Boom Boom Pow" (a big hit a couple of years ago) came on, and I found myself grabbing Cindy's arm and pulling her onto the dance floor. I started break-dancing and doing the robot and spinning on my back like a top. I finally got off the floor when the booing got too loud, but I didn't care—my clothes didn't fall off, they didn't smell, and they didn't even have any stains on them.

That is, until my mom asked me to hold her full glass of punch while she took about four hundred pictures of Cindy and me. Cindy reached for my hand, and I spilled the whole cup of punch, nailing my pants, shirt, and shoes. I think even my socks turned pink.

My mom's photo albums from the dance.

The truth was, I had a lot more fun at the dance than I ever imagined. I figured I should thank Arnie for pushing me to go, for getting me to ask Cindy Shano in the hallway that day. I had been so busy suspecting Arnie of going behind my back with Ryan, I forgot to appreciate that he looks out for me.

I checked all around the dance and didn't see Arnie anywhere. Suddenly, Garth walked over and gave me a kind of evil grin. "You lookin' for Arnie, Cartboy? Try behind the bleachers."

I thought Garth was playing a trick on me, but since I didn't see Arnie anywhere else, I walked past the bleachers. That's when I saw the four legs.

Two for Arnie. And two for Ryan Horner.

I stopped dead in my tracks and peered into the back of the bleachers just in time to see Arnie's fingers punch something in his phone. Then he passed the phone over to Ryan.

Ryan smiled.

There was only one thing on Arnie's phone

that Ryan would want to read. Our secret. The series of movements Susie must do *after* she gets the scythe.

"Fair trade?" I heard Ryan say to Arnie.

"Fair," Arnie answered.

As Arnie started to walk away, he almost stepped on my feet. "What exactly are you trading, Arn?" I asked.

"Hal, I was just about to come find you. I traded . . ."

"Save it. I know what you traded. The only thing we have over Ryan. The one thing. Our secret. It's good to know whose side you're on."

"But I gave him—"

"Forget it, Arnie. You're a traitor. I'll get to the next level by myself."

"You better watch who you're calling a traitor!" I heard Arnie shout as I stormed out of the dance and into the freezing cold night. I walked home by myself, and my clothes didn't make me feel so great anymore.

As I'm writing this, I can't help but wonder if

in the future times you live in people have BFs or BFFs. Maybe you have BFs to the nth degree because you probably figured out what infinity is by now.

I hope in the times you live in, that when it comes to friends, kids spread themselves out instead of having just one.

That's what I recommend.

Because when you don't, it just leads to trouble.

"Just shake out the blood + teeth and it'll be fine."

"Argggh! Me peg leg will serve thee well."

18,592 B.C.   620 B.C.   529 A.D.   1247   1540

"I only pooped in it twice, grog."

"These are all the rage in Sparta!"

"These boots will be all the rage again some day. They'll be called UGGS."

Over Time

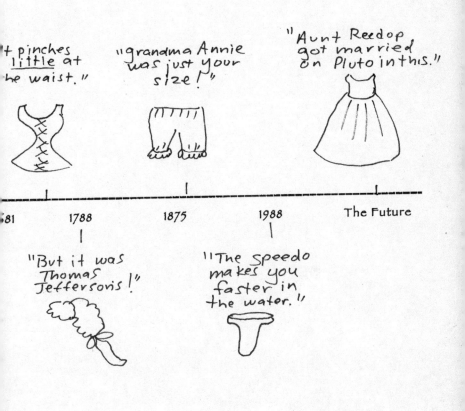

Volunteering

Dear Harry/Bob/Sally/Josh/Zringldorp/Kirzbop:

These days, schools like to organize volunteer programs. The sixth grade science teacher, Mrs. Weiss, runs ours and it's called Kids Pitchin' In. Everyone has to participate. It's part of our grade.

"When it comes to giving your time to a good cause, it's important to choose something close to your heart," Mrs. Weiss said.

My *former* best friend, Arnie, immediately raised his hand. "I'll supervise the girls' locker room." (The place where girls get changed for gym. Gross.)

Mrs. Weiss ignored Arnie's remark and pointed to Hilary Valentine.

"I'll help take care of dogs at the shelter," she said.

The shelter is where animals try to look cute so you'll adopt them.

"Very good, Hilary! Who's next?"

The rest of the kids offered to pick up litter on the sides of highways and nearby beaches and parks and stuff like that. I guess a lot of volunteer projects with kids involve cleaning up other people's messes.

Before I knew it, everyone had picked something except me. I thought about it a lot on the way home from school, and at dinner I told my parents my idea. "I will nobly volunteer to test video games," I said. "Someone has to do it."

They shot that idea down in about four seconds.

Which was annoying because I had no other ideas. Something from my heart? What else could that be?

The day after the assignment, I walked to school and saw lots of kids cleaning the parks and playgrounds and sides of the roads. It freaked me out even more that I still hadn't picked a project.

I was feeling especially lousy when I got to Mr. Tupkin's class, but then I noticed a flyer sitting on his desk.

And that was when the lightbulb went on in my head. Couldn't something from my heart also be something that would land me a good grade? Pass history? Get me my own room?

Couldn't they be one and the same thing?

While Mr. Tupkin was writing on the blackboard, I scribbled the phone number from the brochure on the back of my hand. As soon as I got home, I called.

"Stowfield Historical Society," said a woman who sounded about a hundred and fifty years old.

"Hi. My name is Hal Rifkind. I'm calling about volunteering."

"How old are you?"

"Twelve."

"Would you like to be part of this week's History Night?"

"Sure! I just love history!"

I figured, how hard could it be to scrub down a couple of colonial butter churners, or shine a few Indian arrowheads?

"What's your specialty?" asked Grandma Moses.

"Well, my mom says to dust first and then vacuum, and I pretty much agree with that."

There was a lot of silence at the end of the line, but eventually the lady said, "Well, here's how it works. You will get ten minutes. And you can do whatever you want. Whatever interests you most. Please read the guidelines in the flyer, and if you have any questions don't hesitate to call."

"Sounds great."

"See you at eight o'clock Thursday night. Oh, and one last thing. Bring your own materials, please."

I wasn't sure exactly what materials they needed, but just to be on the safe side, I grabbed a mop, a bucket, and some furniture polish called Lemon Pledge. According to the commercials, "You can dust, clean, and shine all at once."

I thought about reading the instructions in the brochure, but I figured, why bother? Cleaning is cleaning, right?

On Thursday night, I loaded up the cart with my supplies and walked across town toward the Historical Society. When I got there, I was surprised to see how full the parking lot was. But then I realized, with a crowd this size, they were probably going to need a good scrub-down. Maybe history buffs were secretly party animals, and there would be broken lamps and stuff.

No one was in the reception area when I walked in, so I just kind of stood there and looked around. The place was filled with old, dusty stuff, that's for sure. There were maps and compasses and bear skins everywhere.

Ten minutes? I was supposed to speak about history for ten minutes to a packed house at the Historical Society? What was I thinking? Why didn't I read that brochure?

I was about to run out the front door, but then wouldn't you know it, Mr. Tupkin appeared in front of me.

"Quite a shock to see you here, Mr. Rifkind." He straightened his bow tie and gave me a hard look. "Somehow this is the last place I thought you would volunteer." He let out a big sigh, like he knew he was wasting his breath. "I'll lead you to the podium."

As it turns out, just about every important person who lives in Stowfield is a member of the Historical Society. Mayor Sheffield. The entire police department. Mr. Tupkin and about half the teachers at Stowfield Middle School.

From the back of the room, Grampa Janson gave me a salute.

Mr. Tupkin cleared his throat, faced the crowd, and said, "Ladies and gentlemen, I'd like to introduce tonight's first youth volunteer, my student Hal Rifkind."

There was a loud round of applause. When it died down, I grabbed on to my mop for life support.

Silence.

"Um. Ahhh. History is . . . the unconscious attempt to bring the past to the future and learn, um . . ."

More silence.

"Or . . . I should say . . . the man who does not learn from the past is self-conscious about the future."

Fourteen minutes and forty seconds to go.

"I mean, if you look at history, especially early history, it goes way back. In time."

Mr. Tupkin gave me a look that said he might

run up there and strangle me right in front of the mayor.

I held up the can of Lemon Pledge for all the crowd to see. "To a time before you could dust, clean, and shine all at once."

Before I was asked to leave the podium, I managed to kill about five minutes talking about the sponge mop and the bucket—two of man's most highly evolved tools. I did get a few claps from a couple of ladies in the audience who probably had neat homes and appreciated the visual aids.

You can avoid buying a mop
if you have the right kind of dog.

Out in the parking lot I started to load up the cart with my cleaning supplies, when I looked up to see Mr. Tupkin standing right next to me. "That was a disgrace," he said.

"I know. It was a mistake. I was confused . . ."

"What is your problem with history, anyway, Mr. Rifkind?"

I must have been tired or embarrassed or just plain mad, because I'm not sure what came over me next. I looked Mr. Tupkin right in the eyes, and said, "My problem with history is that it's boring. And you make it even more boring than it already is. Which is practically impossible. Because history is the *most boring* thing on the planet!"

"I'm lowering your grade one letter for that little outburst."

"Go ahead! What difference does it make anyway?" I shouted.

I grabbed the cart and yanked the handles so hard the last little bits of rubber popped off. As I squeaked across the parking lot, away from Mr. Tupkin, away from that horrible Historical

Society, the squeaking got so loud I could barely hear myself think. Stupid cart. What good was it? Lugging all those books around for most of sixth grade and what did it get me? I had a failing grade. No best friend. And a nickname I wouldn't shake for a hundred years.

I squeaked my way across town, and with every block I got closer to my house, the more I wished things were different. The more I wished I had a dad who didn't care so much about history. Who would just let it go, cut me a break. If I did have a dad like that, none of this would have happened.

After what seemed like forever, I made it to my street. I pulled up to my driveway and was about to go inside. But then I pictured the look on my dad's face when he found out my new grade, and a thought occurred to me. Maybe, instead of going home, I would swing by Arnie's first. Whatever Arnie had done, I figured, we had stuck with each other since we were two. I was sure we could work it out. Besides, I was probably wrong about Susie and the scythe. The whole thing had to be some big misunderstanding. Arnie wouldn't trade our secret without telling me.

The main thing though, I have to admit, was that after getting chewed out by Mr. Tupkin, I could've really used a friend.

I went up to Arnie's house and saw the light on in the basement. Rather than get pummeled by Garth at the front door, I thought I'd peek in the basement window and whisper Arnie's name.

But I didn't even get that far. The first thing I saw when I looked through the window was Arnie sitting in front of the television screen. He was playing RavenCave. And he had reached the next level. Susie was holding the scythe.

Arnie had found it by himself. Actually, I take that back. He had help. Ryan was standing near the basement door. He was drinking a Gatorade, watching Arnie play, and laughing.

I walked away from the window and headed the other direction. There was no place to go but home.

How Kids Have Volunteere

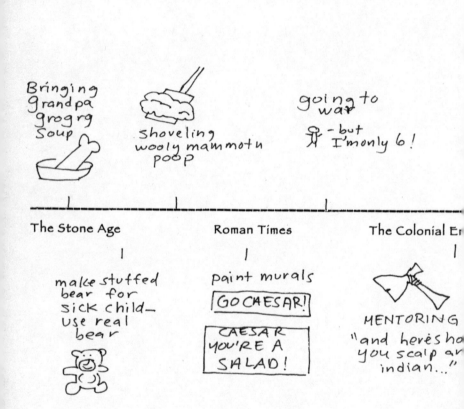

Bringing
grandpa
grog rg
Soup

shoveling
wooly mammoth
poop

going to
war
– but
I'm only 6!

The Stone Age

make stuffed
bear for
sick child—
use real
bear

Roman Times

paint murals

GO CAESAR!

CAESAR
YOU'RE A
SALAD!

The Colonial Er

MENTORING
"and here's ho
you scalp ar
indian..."

hrough the Ages

whee!

tea party
clean-up

Pick up
soda cans
in space

Revolutionary War Times | The Present | The Future

sell 200 boxes
of girl scout
cookies.
Or else!

THIN
MINTS

Punishment

Dear Life-Form That's Way More
Advanced Than Me:

It occurred to me that in the time it's taken you to read this far, you might have gotten access to a time machine. And I was thinking, if you *have* come across a time machine, and if it's not too much trouble, would you mind beaming me up to the future sooner rather than later? Because the thing is, I have to *get out of here right this second*.

If you're wondering what the emergency is, it's just that, let me think of how to put this. Oh, yeah. *I'm a dead man.*

Seriously, if you can get me out of here, you will be saving a boy's life.

Why is that boy in so much danger, you ask. I've got one letter for you.

F

That's what my history grade is now.

Mr. Tupkin wasn't kidding about lowering it a whole grade, and he made sure to call my parents right away. He said there was one month of school left and I was failing.

"Hal, get in the kitchen right now!" yelled my dad.

"Things just got a little out of control, Dad. How about if I make it up to you?" I held up the mop. "I could do some cleaning . . . ?"

"No son of mine will fail history," he said. "History is who we are and why."

"Dad, I'll never pass. Even if there was a miracle and I did okay on the final exam, Mr. Tupkin hates me now. It's a lost cause. So you can save the dumb quotes."

"Dumb quotes. Is that what you think they are? Dumb?"

"Yes, dumb!"

"It is history, Hal, that keeps the mistakes of the past from entering the present."

I guess you could call that one "the quote that broke the camel's back." Because I completely lost it and before I knew it, I was screaming at my dad.

"That's exactly what I mean! You always say stuff like 'History keeps you from making the same mistakes. Blah blah.' But look at you! You make the same mistakes over and over. Like, forcing me to take an old-lady cart to school. And being the one dad in the entire town that never ever gets anything new. You act like your only purpose in life is to learn history. But it's not. It's to embarrass me! You're one big, dusty, squeaky, grease monkey of a mistake."

"That's it, mister," my dad yelled. "You will study, and study hard you will. Go to your room and don't come out until you've memorized the entire Declaration of Independence."

"What?! That thing's like three hundred pages long!"

"In your room, now! You're grounded."

The funny thing is that my dad kept saying, "*Your* room. Get in *your* room." As if!

I ran out of the kitchen, into "my" room, and slammed the door. My hands were shaking, and I was out of breath, so I sat down on my bed between the cribs. That was by far the biggest fight I've ever had with my dad, and we've had a couple of doozies.

I guess I shouldn't have slammed the door so hard, because the twins woke up. They looked like they were working themselves up for a good cry, but then for some reason they stayed quiet. It was almost like they knew I was at the end of my rope. Like I said, babies are probably a lot smarter than we think.

But still, they poop and pee in their pants. So I spent the next couple of hours changing diapers and reading the Declaration of Independence at the same time. Okay, I was relieved to see it was only one page long. But memorizing those twelve hundred words is about as fun as getting thrown into Wolfie's pen by Ryan and Garth.

When in the course of human events it becomes necessary blah de blah blah . . .

We hold these truths to be self-evident, that all men are created equal gluggety blah blaggedy zzzzzz . . .

I did perk up when I got to the part that said, "there shall be no cruel and unusual punishment," because at that moment, Bea spit up on my computer.

Normally, during times like this, when I'm grounded or stuck studying for a hard test, Arnie would sneak up to my window and pass me a chocolate-glazed doughnut with sprinkles. That night, while staring at the Declaration of Independence, I glanced out the window every now and then. Maybe it was out of habit, maybe I was hoping that even though Arnie went behind my back with Ryan, he would still come by.

But he didn't.

I looked over at the twins with their rattles and blankets and stuffed animals. Their lives seemed so simple. If only there was a simple solution for getting out of the mess I was in.

Any sort of molecule melter, nano-particle transformer, or time-travel contraption will do.

The Light Tripper

Space Ride

The Milky way Express

The Blowback

What??

Activities

Dear Person Of The Future Who May Or May Not
Speak English, In Which Case This Whole Journal
Probably Looks Like This—Xhjoif Nwm OenfWhtzq
Wyasfwrewoiulkn Lbgcde Lnieuekenr Mffwf:

I am still here, so thanks anyway about the time
machine. I guess that was just wishful thinking
on my part, but I do hope they make one some-
day and that I am around when they do.

By the looks of things, I'm going to be
grounded forever. There's just four weeks left of
sixth grade and my dad is mad as ever.

Which totally stinks because summer is almost here and, as I mentioned before, I do not
have access to:

RavenCave

Phillies, Flyers, Eagles

Hanging with Arnie

(Even though, technically, since the night of the dance, Arnie and I still haven't spoken. If we spot each other coming down the hallway, we each pretend to have something stuck in our fingernail, or an itch on our eye, or something like that.)

The worst part of being grounded is that the chance of me getting a room where I don't have to sleep between two baby girls is now around zero percent. And I don't see any way out. My dad is so mad he can barely look at me. I'm not sure if he ever will again.

Mr. Tupkin will barely look at me either. So he's *definitely* a lost cause. (I wrote him an apology letter, for saying he was boring and all, but I'm pretty sure he didn't even read it.)

Given the situation, I have had no choice but to take matters into my own hands. To come up with a Plan B.

Besides my dad and Mr. Tupkin, there's just one other person who can get me ungrounded. One last person who could overlook a lousy little F for the happiness of a young man. A person who is still, on the inside anyway, a great big mush.

Mom.

My idea is to do some good old-fashioned, time-honored, sucking up to the lady of the house. Do stuff with her that she likes to do. Help out. Make eye contact with her friends.

Which is why I'm going to tell you about a few activities that are a really *big deal,* especially with moms, on Earth right now.

#1 ACTIVITY THAT IS
REALLY BIG ON EARTH TODAY:
THE BOOK CLUB

There is barely a mom alive today who is not part of something called "book club."

For reasons my brain can't begin to process, once a month they all get together at someone's house to discuss a book they have read *for fun*. Not because they had to read the book, but because they *wanted to*.

One thing I noticed is that whenever my mom hosts the book club, she puts out about fifty trays of little snacks and cookies and stuff. I guess all that reading makes you hungry.

The month of May is always my mom's turn to host. When the ladies showed up at seven o'clock last Tuesday night, I was ready.

They all gathered in the living room and started to chat about the book they were reading, *Sense and Sensibility*. (A super barfy love story by someone named Jane Austen.) As soon as the conversation got going, I appeared in the doorway with a tray of oval-shaped vanilla cookies.

"Ladyfinger, anyone?"

Ladyfinger cookies.

Ladyfinger cookies you could make on Halloween.

I'd put on my mom's apron for extra effect, and as I passed the tray around, I made sure to stop at every one of the ladies.

"Here you go, Mrs. Boswell. How's your knee? Better I hope."

"Mrs. Stoddard! You're looking ravishing!"

"Well, hello, Mrs. Popper. I can hardly notice the hair in your mole tonight."

When I reached my mom with the cookie tray, she gave me a long stare. Her eyebrows got that crinkle in between them like they always do when she gets mad. But when she heard Mrs. Boswell and Mrs. Stoddard talking about what a nice boy I was, I saw her melt like a fudge pop in the sun.

Before leaving the room, I casually grabbed a copy of *Sense and Sensibility* off the coffee table. "I don't know about you all," I said, "but I believe the main character, Marianna, was correct in believing one should marry for love, not for money or position."

Thank God for book summaries on the Internet.

I tossed the book on the table and walked out holding my ladyfingers high. Check, I thought, on the book club.

What's next?

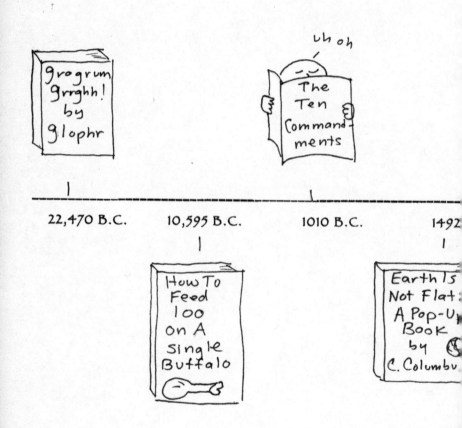

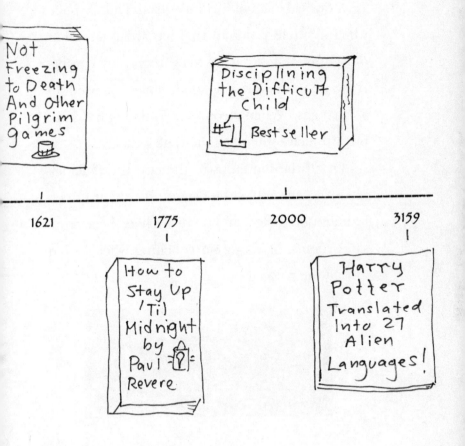

Not Freezing to Death And Other Pilgrim games

Disciplining the Difficult Child
#1 Bestseller

1621   1775   2000   3159

How to Stay Up 'Til Midnight by Paul Revere

Harry Potter Translated Into 27 Alien Languages!

#2 ACTIVITY THAT IS
REALLY BIG ON EARTH TODAY:
THE ART MUSEUM

Stowfield is about fifty miles from Philadelphia, which is a really old city that has about a million museums. Whenever we drive there, my parents try to cram in every single one since "we used up all that gas." When it comes to Philadelphia, I am pretty much sobbing by the time we leave.

Of all the museums in the city, the Philadelphia Art Museum is the biggest. It's about fifteen jazillion square feet and there are like, three thousand rooms. My body starts aching when I even look at the place.

The Philadelphia Art Museum,
known to kids everywhere as the "Museum of Pain."

176

But my mom loves all museums, the bigger and artier the better. So a few days ago, when she was making lentil soup, I dropped by the kitchen.

"Hi, Mom. I was thinking, I'd like to spend some more time with you."

"That's nice, honey."

"How about a day at the Philadelphia Art Museum? Just you and me?"

"Are you feeling okay?"

"Yeah, Mom, I just am really becoming interested in art. Maybe you could show me some stuff you like."

"I'd love to! Let's go tomorrow. Admission is free on Sundays in May and the museum is open until five o'clock. We can stay for six hours!"

"Six hours?"

"I mean, uh . . . that's great!"

I tried to keep from crumpling onto the kitchen floor. "Sounds like a nice day together, Mom."

I could already tell this was going to be much, much harder than the book club. Six hours of looking at paintings and sculptures and little Chinese vases. They have a whole wing just on needlepoint rugs!

But as my dad always likes to say, "Desperate times call for desperate measures."

The museum doors opened at 11:00 A.M. sharp and my mom charged in there like a Thoroughbred out of the starting gate. "Where should we start? Ooohh, how about nineteenth-century decorative arts? No, let's do French Impressionism."

By noon, I thought I was going to die and we still had five hours to go.

"Oh, Hal, look at the craftsmanship in that ceramic figurine!"

"It's exquisite, Mom."

"C'mon, let's head over to the lecture on Roman Aqueducts."

My mom trotted from room to room, with me slugging along behind her, trying to keep my legs from buckling and my eyes from sticking shut. The only thing that kept me going was the hope that every hour I spent with her was one hour closer to being ungrounded.

That, and a few of the sculptures were pretty entertaining.

At some point late in the afternoon, my mom and I walked into the Hall of Egyptian Tombs. It was full of all these stone slabs and burial treasures the Egyptians made a long time ago. They had so many complicated carvings, it must've taken them a hundred years to build each one.

Given how much work it was just to rebuild a little deck railing, I could appreciate what the Egyptians went through. I practically broke out in a sweat just looking at those tombs.

I was kind of lost in this thought when I looked over, and who did I see standing right in front of the tombs?

Ryan Horner.

What was he doing at the museum? It didn't make any sense. Then I noticed he was sketching one of the giant stone slabs. He must have had to come here for history homework.

Suddenly, I really *was* breaking out in a sweat. The last time I saw Ryan, he was at the top of Arnie's basement stairs laughing. Seeing him again made me so mad I wanted to shove him into one of those stone coffins and shut the lid. But if I tried to do anything like that, he'd just stand there and yell something like, "Nice try, Cartboy." Or, "Maybe next time, Cartboy."

The best thing I could do was get out of there as fast as I could, before he spotted me. I steered my mom in the opposite direction, but right as we were leaving the room, something caught my eye. Ryan was texting on Arnie's phone. I could tell because of the custom purple plaid case.

What the heck was Ryan doing with Arnie's phone? Did he steal it? Did Arnie let him borrow it? I thought back to the night of the dance, when I saw Arnie and Ryan behind the bleachers. Arnie had definitely shown Ryan something on his phone. It *had* to be our secret.

But now, Ryan had the phone. The whole thing was making my head spin, because all I know is that Arnie's phone is his favorite thing in the world, so why would Ryan have it?

The question gnawed at me right up until about five o'clock, when it was finally time to go home. My head was aching, my feet were on fire, and my back was killing me from all that walking.

I looked a lot like Uncle Lou.

In one way, though, it had been a good day. I could tell I was close to getting ungrounded. We walked toward the car, and my mom put her arm over my shoulder. "You want to go for ice cream, honey?" she said. "There's a place just a few blocks from here."

It worked! It worked! I thought. She's taking me for ice cream! I'm out of the doghouse!

My mom and I sat down at the ice-cream counter and started to eat our whole-wheat soy cones. After a minute, she looked up and stared me right in the eye. Here it comes, I thought. She's going to tell me I'm ungrounded.

Instead, all she said was, "I know what you're doing."

"What do you mean, Mom? Do you want to go to the green market after this?"

"I love that you are trying to get on my good side, Hal. To be a better son."

"Um . . ."

"But there's only one way to get out of being grounded. It's time to forget about me. And do the thing you *should* be doing."

Unfortunately, I knew exactly what she was talking about. Studying for the history final. It was in two weeks, right before the end of school.

"I can't learn history, Mom. I just don't get it."

"Why don't you talk to Dad?"

Suddenly, my whole-wheat soy cone didn't taste so good. Even though it was sugary and sweet, it left a bitter taste in my mouth. I figured it probably had nothing to do with the ice cream. And everything to do with the fact that my mom might be right.

Popular Tourist Attraction

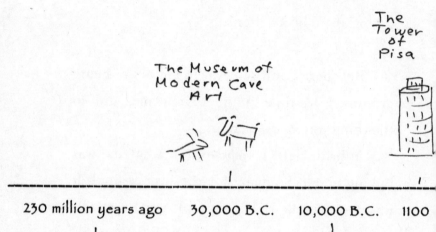

The Museum of Modern Cave Art

The Tower of Pisa

230 million years ago · 30,000 B.C. · 10,000 B.C. · 1100

The Museum of Dinosaurs Still Alive

The Loin Cloth Museum

Must Be Over 18

hrough The Ages

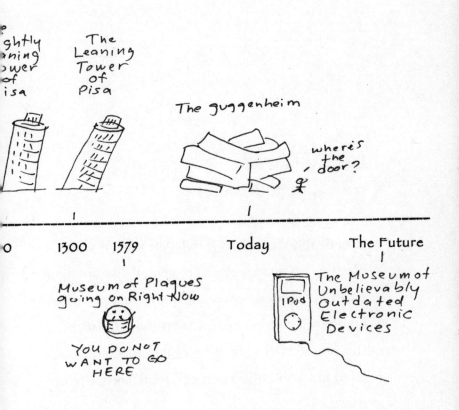

ghtly
ining
ɔwer
of
isa

The
Leaning
Tower
of
Pisa

The guggenheim

where's
the
door?

0   1300   1579   Today   The Future

Museum of Plaques
going on Right Now

YOU DO NOT
WANT TO GO
HERE

iPod

The Museum of
Unbelievably
Outdated
Electronic
Devices

Dear Whoever Found This Journal
and Has Actually Made It This Far:

I really didn't want to talk to my dad. It seemed like the worst idea ever. It seemed like my dad and I had gotten to a point where we were never going to see eye to eye on anything. I didn't have the remotest clue how two people could be related but also be 100 percent, total, complete opposites.

But in the end, that was the thing that changed my mind. I realized my dad is my dad and we couldn't go on not speaking to each other forever. Even though I was sure the talk wouldn't go well, I figured I should give it a try.

I found him sitting quietly at our kitchen table, sewing a button on a ragged blue uniform. He was getting ready to do his favorite hobby, Revolutionary War reenacting. He and his friends go over to the soccer field in town where they act like they're at Bunker Hill taking on the British. They pretend to shoot one another, then head over to Arby's for a snack afterward.

Arby's roast beef sandwich with "horsey sauce." No one knows which part of the horsey the sauce comes from.

"Dad?" I said.

He didn't look up.

"Dad, I'm sorry I called you a grease monkey."

He still didn't look up.

"And that I said you were dusty. And squeaky. And . . . I'm sorry I said your quotes are dumb."

I waited for him to talk, but he just sat there sewing and not saying anything at all. Things were going even worse than I thought they would.

"It's just . . . the thing is . . . I'm having the most horrible year ever. It's not only because I don't like, okay hate, history. It's . . . well . . . Arnie went behind my back. I never thought Arnie was perfect, but turns out he's not the person I thought he was. At all. And now, sixth grade is almost over, and I don't even have a friend. I guess I kind of took my frustrations out on you."

Finally, my dad lifted up his head. He put down his sewing needle and looked me straight in the eye. "When I was your age, I had a tough time in history too. I just didn't see why it was so important."

The words "history" and "not important" had never appeared together in one of my dad's sentences before.

"But then, how come you think history is so interesting now?" I asked. "I mean, all the people are still dead. And the facts are just as boring."

"That's true. History *is* about a bunch of dead people. And I agree that the dates and the battles and the treaties and stuff can all seem the same. But that's not all there is to history."

My dad reached under the table and started feeling around for something on one of the kitchen chairs. I heard a crinkling noise, then I saw him pull out a shopping bag. It didn't look like the usual ratty old shopping bags we have around the house. There were no worn-out handles or rips in the bottom. I wasn't sure, but it seemed like a brand-new shopping bag from Binders, the bookstore downtown.

"I got you something," he said.

And then, my dad reached in the bag and pulled out a book. As he did, I noticed something

I hadn't seen in a long, long time. My dad was holding a cash-register receipt. The book he got me was brand new.

"Yes, it is a history book, Hal. But I promise it's not boring. It's a bunch of short stories about the most famous men of the Revolutionary War. George Washington. Benjamin Franklin. Benedict Arnold. Guys who did amazing things."

I took the book from him and ran my hand along the shiny cover.

"I think you'll find the stories of all these men interesting. They weren't perfect. They made a lot of bad decisions. But they made good decisions too. Decisions that still affect our lives today."

I saw that the book had tons of pictures and the words were big. It was like it was written for kids who don't like history.

"This book really helped me when I was your age. I think it'll help you too. You might even come across something in these stories that'll lead you to the thing you're looking for most," said my dad. "Right now. In sixth grade."

"Dad, the thing I'm really looking for, the thing I'm dying to find, is in RavenCave. It's Susie's scythe. There's no way this book could help me with that."

"You never know."

Dear John? Sally? Ben? Hzimaloo? Zringelop?

For the past two weeks, I've studied and studied and studied. Every day. History, history, history.

For the entire first half of June, I got Cindy Shano to come over after school and tutor me. It was pure torture and cost me about a year's allowance in Milk Duds, but after a while some of the stuff actually started to stick.

Thomas Paine's pamphlet "Common Sense" inspired people to fight for their freedom.

Paul Revere's midnight ride warned the colonists the British were about to attack.

George Washington convinced nearly all his troops in Trenton to keep fighting for independence, even though they were tired, hungry, cold, and legally allowed to go home.

Benedict Arnold decided to switch loyalties and side with the British. He deserted the Patriot army.

There were lots and lots of facts. So many facts. In the end, it was impossible to remember all of them. All I can say is, I tried.

That last fact, though, the one about Benedict Arnold, kept sticking in my brain. Partly because of the book my dad gave me. And partly for an even bigger reason—I could understand first-hand what it meant to be a traitor. What it was like to ditch a loyal friend and go to the other side. 'Cause that's pretty much what I did to Arnie.

It turns out Arnie *had* given Ryan something valuable to get the answer to how Susie could find the scythe. But it wasn't our secret that he traded. The thing he traded was his phone. Cindy told me while we were studying. Just about everyone in the whole school knew about it besides me.

Arnie gave Ryan his favorite possession so he could get the secret not for himself, but for both of us. So we could get to Level 13 together, like we'd always planned.

I haven't seen Arnie much lately. I looked over in his direction once in Mr. Tupkin's class, but he looked the other way. If I had to guess, I'd say he's got himself a new best friend by now.

Right after I finished taking the history final,

I went straight home. I sat down on my bed next to Bea and Perrie and opened up RavenCave on my computer. I was still stuck on Level 12. The only difference was that finally I knew how to get to Level 13. I didn't have any special tips or secrets or ideas. I just knew that I was going to have to fight hard to find the answer, and not give up until I got it. I also knew that when I got to Level 13, I wasn't going to stop. I would keep going until I reached Level 14. That way, if Arnie does ever speak to me again, I can show him how to get there too.

Believe it or not, almost a whole school year has gone by since I first started writing to you. This is going to be my last communication because we have to hand in our journals to Mr. Tupkin tomorrow.

I hope somehow I helped you see what life was like long before you lived.

And that wherever you're from, it is a good place. Where they have easy tests, a video game as good as RavenCave, and tons of doughnuts. If they do, *definitely* try the chocolate-glazed with sprinkles.

Sincerely,

Hal

Goodbye, So Long, Zip Dop Snorg!

I'm sneaking this one last bit in at the end because I wanted to tell you what happened today, on the last day of school.

I got the score of my history final.

I barely, just barely passed.

I actually worked really hard and was glad I passed the test. But I was also pretty bummed because there was no way my score was high enough to make me pass for the year.

The last person I wanted to see was Mr. Tupkin. I avoided him all day. But when eighth period rolled around, I had no choice. I needed to turn in my history textbooks and clean out my locker.

I walked into the history classroom, and Mr. Tupkin was sitting there alone. He was behind his desk, reading a dusty old book. He didn't even look up when I walked over. So I just dropped the textbooks in the pile near his desk and turned to leave.

I stopped when I heard Mr. Tupkin say, "Hal." He never calls me that.

"I want to tell you your final grade for the year."

I turned around to face him. I noticed my throat was dry and my palms had started to feel clammy.

"That's okay, Mr. Tupkin, I'll just wait for the report card."

"No. I think you should know."

Mr. Tupkin rubbed his bow tie, looked at me

with this kind of sad face, and then he said, "I'm giving you a C plus."

"But . . . I barely passed the final exam."

"I know."

"And I almost failed the midterm."

"I know."

"I gave a lecture on Lemon Pledge at the Historical Society."

"Don't remind me."

"You mean . . . you actually don't hate me?"

"Hal, it's not about whether I like you or not. If there is one thing, just one thing you learn from my history class, it's that most of those people in the history books are there because they stood up to someone and spoke their mind."

The funny thing was, I think I understood what Mr. Tupkin was saying.

"But there's another reason I'm giving you a C plus. I read your time-capsule journal. It was . . . not bad."

He actually said *not* bad.

"Those timelines, though. They were ridiculous. I mean, really, monkeys dancing on Mars?"

"Yeah, I guess that was pretty silly. But, it's possible? Isn't it?"

"One of the most famous history quotes of all time is by a man named Voltaire. He said, 'History consists of a series of accumulated imaginative inventions.'"

"I'm sorry, Mr. Tupkin, I have no idea what that means."

"It means yes. It's possible."

Voltaire   Lead singer of
                  the band Voltaire

(I'm pretty sure Mr. Tupkin was talking
about the guy on the left.)

At the end of the day, I ran into Arnie by our lockers. He was talking to Heather Fukumoto. I'm not sure, but I could swear he was already making plans for next year's middle school dance.

"Hey, Arnie," I said.

Arnie turned from Heather to me, but he didn't say a word.

"It's okay, Arnie. You don't have to say anything. I was an idiot, so I totally get why we're not friends anymore. But I wanted to tell you how to get to Level Fourteen on RavenCave. It's the least I could do."

I explained to Arnie that you have to take Susie and her scythe into an even bigger cave where she battles humongous bats, eels with giant jaws, and the stalagmite witch.

"It's hard. Really hard," I said. "But it's doable. You just have to make sure Susie keeps the scythe with her all the time. And that she never lets go."

Arnie walked over, put his arms around me, and gave me a manpat.

"I should have told you what I was doing with Ryan, Hal. I guess I wanted it to be a surprise. Sorry."

I could tell that Arnie had forgiven me for calling him a traitor. And that he and I were gonna go back to being best friends.

Sure, maybe he'd still chase after girls. And he'd probably get another phone, and talk for hours in front of me like he always does. But it was better than the opposite: no Arnie at all, no having a friend who knows you better than anyone else. Like, for example, right that very second, even though I didn't say anything, he could tell something was wrong.

"What's the matter?" he asked.

"I got a C plus in history."

"You don't seem too happy about it."

"I am. But, it's just that my dad is still saying I need a B to get my own room."

"Well Hal, I've got a little history quote of my own to tell you. Goes something like this:

Throughout the ages, whenever a kid has wanted his own room, a little begging never hurt."

I heard what Arnie was saying, and I decided to take his advice. As soon as I got home from school, I went into the spare room where my dad was fixing a blender.

"Hey, Dad?" I asked. "Even though I didn't get a B in history, do you think there's a *chance* I could get my own room?"

"I'll think about it."

"How about if Arnie and I finish building the shed this summer?"

Suddenly, my dad looked up at me with a serious look on his face. "I'm not sure you're going to have time to build a shed this summer."

"Well, there's no school for three months. Seems like plenty of time to me. I mean, it's not like I'll be bogged down with lots of history homework or anything. . . ."

I smiled, but the look on my dad's face got even *more* serious, and my smile went away fast.

"I don't think this summer is going to be exactly what you're expecting, Hal."

"But . . . you agree that summer is for relaxing, giving the old brain some time to recharge. Right, Dad?"

My dad put his hand on a piece of paper that was sticking out of the pocket of his work shirt. I couldn't tell exactly what the paper was. But I could swear there were some words in colonial-looking letters on the front.

"Right, Dad?" I asked again, trying to hide the quiver in my voice.

But all he said was, "We'll see, Hal. We'll see."

Acknowledgments

Thank you, Beau and Charlie, for contributing so much. This book is yours too.

Dad, Mom, Yve, Rob, Cara, Duff, Lynn, Greg, Aida, Allison, Jamie, Monica, Anna, Hilary, Griff, Steffani, Sintra, Wendy, Frances, Eve, Peter, Leo, Lynn B., Jill, Alison, Heather, Stacy, Maddie, Dave, Jan, and Ian—thank you for all your help and support.

Thank you, Laura Dail and Susan Chang. It's an honor to work with you both.

And thank you to Bianca Howell, who never gave up and inspired me to do the same.

About the Author

L. A. Campbell grew up in Park Ridge, New Jersey, and attended the University of Colorado, graduating with a degree in journalism. She started her own ad agency, which won awards for work on such brands as Comedy Central and *New York* magazine. *Cartboy and the Time Capsule* is her first book. She lives in New York City with her husband and two children.